DEATH SHOT

McCluskie's knees buckled and he was suddenly gripped with the urgency of killing Anderson ... He heard the gunfire and the terrified shrieks of dance-hall girls, sensed the crowd scattering. But it was all somehow distant, even a little unreal. Blinded, falling swiftly into darkness, he willed his hand to move. To finish what he had come here to do.

Another bullet smacked him in the ribs, but like a dead snake, operating on nerves alone, his hand reacted and came up with the Colt. That he couldn't see Anderson bothered him not at all. In his mind's eye he remembered exactly where the Texan was standing, and even as he pressed the trigger, he knew the shot had struck home ...

"MATT BRAUN IS ONE OF THE BEST!"
—Don Coldsmith, author of the Spanish Bit series

"HE TELLS IT STRAIGHT—AND HE TELLS IT WELL."
—Jory Sherman, author of *Grass Kingdom*

KINCH RILEY

(Previously published as *Kinch*)

MATT BRAUN

St. Martin's Paperbacks

Kinch Riley was previously published under the title *Kinch*.

KINCH RILEY

Copyright © 1975 by Matthew Braun.

ISBN: 0-312-97414-0

Printed in the United States of America

Ace edition / May 1978
St. Martin's Paperbacks edition / June 2000

St. Martin's Paperbacks are published by St. Martin's Press, 175 Fifth Avenue, New York, N.Y. 10010.

10 9 8 7 6 5 4 3 2 1

For
JTA
A Kindred Spirit
Who Was Always There

AUTHOR'S NOTE

This is an epitaph for Kinch Riley.

Essentially it is a true story, gleaned from musty newspaper archives and the chronicles of men who were there. The place is Newton, Kansas, during the summer of 1871. On a sweltering August night a gunfight occurred which came to be known as "Newton's General Massacre." According to the *Topeka Daily Commonwealth*, six men died in the space of ninety seconds. Three more were wounded, one of whom was later killed under curious circumstances. Witnesses to the slaughter credited a young boy, known only as Riley, with having accounted for most of the dead.

Kinch Riley is the story of what led to that fateful night in Newton. More significantly, perhaps, it is a reasonably accurate account of how a bond of loyalty came to exist between a lawman and a consumptive youth of seventeen. Certain liberties have been taken with names and events, but *Kinch Riley* nonetheless explores one of the Old West's most enduring mysteries. While supporting details are available regarding events leading to the shootout, little is known of the boy named Riley.

After killing five men he simply vanished from the pages of history.

The enigma of Kinch Riley has confounded Western scholars for better than a hundred years. Though the story which follows is fiction based on facts, it provides one solution to a seemingly unfathomable riddle. Perhaps the only solution.

At last, it lays a ghost to rest.

KINCH
RILEY

ONE

McCluskie swung down off the caboose and stood for a moment surveying the depot. It was painted a dingy green, the same as all Santa Fe depots. Not unlike a hundred others he had seen, it had all the warmth of a freshly scrubbed privy. The only notable difference being that it was newer and bigger. Rails had been laid into Newton less than a week past, and the town had been designated division point. Otherwise, so far as McCluskie could see, there was nothing remarkable about the place. Just another fleabag cowtown that would serve as home base till the end of track shifted west a couple of hundred miles.

Hefting his war-bag, he walked to the end of the platform and paused for a look at Newton. The corners of his mouth quirked and he grunted with surprise. It wasn't Abilene, but it was damn sure more than he had expected. Especially out in the middle of nowhere, with the rails hardly a week old.

Newton was laid out much on the order of all cowtowns. Main Street spraddled the tracks, with the red-light district on the southside and most of the business establishments on the north. Side streets, none of which were more than a block long, branched off of the dusty main thoroughfare. Nearly every building had the high false-front that had become the trademark of Kansas railheads, and the structures looked as if they had been slapped together with spit and poster glue. What amazed McCluskie was not that Newton existed, but that it had sprung from the earth's bowels with such dizzying speed.

He dropped the war-bag at his feet and started rolling a smoke. The paper and tobacco took shape in his hands without thought, almost a mechanical ritual born of habit. Searching his vest, he found a sulphurhead and flicked it to life with his thumbnail. Touching flame to cigarette, he took a long draw and let his eyes wander along the street. His inspection was brief, for a well-chucked rock would have hit the town limits in any direction. But little escaped his gaze, and except for the hodge-podge of buildings, there wasn't much to stir his interest.

Whatever Newton had to offer wouldn't be all that different. He'd seen the elephant too many times to expect otherwise. Cards and shady ladies and railhead saloons were the same wherever a man hung his hat. Such things didn't change, they just shifted operations whenever the end of track changed. Most times it seemed they had even hauled along the same batch of customers.

McCluskie stuck the cigarette in his mouth, again hefted the war-bag, and started down the platform steps. Somewhere behind him he heard his name called and turned to find Newt Hansberry, the station master, bearing down on him. He didn't care much for Hansberry and had purposely avoided the depot for just that reason. But then, he was sort of stand-offish about people in general, so it wasn't as if he had anything personal against the man.

"Mike, you ol' scutter!" Hansberry rushed up and commenced pumping his hand like he was trying to raise water. "Where the hell did you spring from?"

"Just pulled in on the cowtown express." McCluskie retrieved his hand and wiped it along the side of his pants.

The station master shot a puzzled glance at the cattle cars, then barfed up an oily chuckle. "Cowtown express! That's rich, Mike. Wait'll I try that on the boys." The laughter slacked off and his brow puckered in an owlish frown. "Say, what's a big mucka-muck like you doing in Newton, anyway? The head office didn't tell me you was comin' out here."

McCluskie's look was wooden, revealing nothing. "Why, Newt, you know how the brass are. They're so busy shufflin' people and trains they don't tell no-body nothin'."

"Yeh, but they don't send the top bull to end of track just for exercise." Hansberry cocked one eye-brow in a crafty smirk. "C'mon, Mike, 'fess up. They sent you out here on some kinda job, didn't they? Something hush-hush."

"Sorry to disappoint you, Newt. They just wanted me to have a looksee. Sorta make sure the division has got all the kinks ironed out. Y'know what I mean?"

Hansberry blinked and nodded, swallowing his next question. What with him being station master, that last part had struck a little close to home. "Sure, Mike. I get your drift. But don't worry, I run a tight operation. Always have."

"Never thought you didn't." McCluskie let it drop there and jerked his thumb back toward the main part of town. "What's the low-down on this dump? Anything happened I ought to know about?"

"Well I ain't seen Jesse James around town if that's what you mean. Course, I don't guess the likes of him would go in for robbin' cattle cars anyways."

"Not likely. That wasn't what I was drivin' at, though. Anybody tried to set himself up as the king-fish yet?"

"Hell, ain't nobody had time. They been too busy gettin' this place built. 'Sides, Newton's not rightly a town anyway. Wichita's the county seat and this here is just a township. Won't never be nothin' else, neither. Leastways till somebody proves it's on the map to stay."

"So I heard."

The station master gave him a guarded look. "Yeh, I guess you would've. Don't s'pose there's much that gets past you boys at the head office."

McCluskie let the question slip past. "What about law? They got anybody ridin' herd on the trailhands?"

"Oh, sure. Some of the sportin' crowd and a few of the storekeepers got themselves appointed to the town board and they pestered Wichita into sendin' a deputy up here permanent. Good thing they did, too. Otherwise them Texans would've hoorawed this place clean down to the ground."

"This lawdog, he anybody I know?"

"Sorta doubt it. Name's Tonk Hazeltine. Some

folks says he's a breed, but he don't look like no Injun I ever saw. Queer kind o' bird, though. Acts like he just drunk some green rotgut and didn't care much for the taste."

"Don't think I ever heard of him. How's he handle himself? Been keepin' the drovers in line?"

"Yeh, what there is of 'em. Y'know the stock-yards have only been built a couple of weeks. We're just now startin' to steal a few herds away from Abilene."

"They'll come, don't worry yourself about that. Before the summer's out we'll have the K&P stewin' in their own juice."

"I 'spect you're right. Leastways I ain't never known the Sante Fe to make no foolish bets."

McCluskie merely nodded, his eyes again drifting to the street. "Understand Belle Siddons is in town."

"Sure is. Got herself a house down on Third Street. I seem to recollect you and her was sorta thick in Abilene."

"You oughtn't to listen so good, Newt." McCluskie flicked his cigarette stub onto the tracks and started down the platform steps. When he reached the bottom, he stopped and looked back. "What's the best hotel in town?"

"Why, I guess that'd be the Newton House. Fanciest digs this side of Kansas City. Just turn north across the tracks and keep goin'. You can't miss it."

McCluskie turned south and headed down the street, walking toward a ramshackle affair that proclaimed itself the National Hotel.

Hansberry watched after him, cursing softly under his breath. There was something about McCluskie that rubbed a man the wrong way. Even if he was head of security for the line. But it wasn't the kind of thing a fellow could put into words. Not out loud anyway.

McCluskie had a certain Gaelic charm about him, with a square jaw and a humorous mouth that was about half covered with a brushy mustache. Yet he was also something of a lone wolf, and damn few men had ever gotten close enough to say they really knew him well. Not that he threw his weight around, or for that matter, even raised his voice. He didn't have to. Most folks just figured he preferred his own company, and they let it go at that.

Part of it, perhaps, had to do with his size. He was a tall man—over six feet—and compactly built. Sledge-shouldered and lean through the hips, he had the look of a prizefighter. Which he might have been at some time in the past. Little was known about him before he showed up in Abilene back in '69. There, working for the Kansas & Pacific, he had killed one man with his fists and a couple more with a gun. After that nobody felt the urge to ask questions.

Yet, as he thought on it, Hansberry was struck by something else entirely. The queer way the Irishman had of looking at a man. Not just cold and unfeeling, but the practiced eyes of a man who stayed alive by making quick estimates. It was sort of unsettling.

The station master watched McCluskie disappear through the door of the hotel, then turned away, muttering to himself. Somehow the day didn't seem so bright any more, but a quick glance at the sky merely confirmed his misgivings. There wasn't a cloud in sight.

* * *

McCluskie came down the hall from his room and entered the lobby. He had shaved, changed to a fresh shirt, and brushed the dust from his suit. His face glowed with a ruddy, weathered vitality, and he was whistling a tuneless ditty to himself. Except for his size and bearing, and the bulge on his right hip, he might have been a spiffy drummer out to sweet-talk the local merchants. As he approached the desk, the room clerk brightened and gave him a flaccid smile.

"Yessir, Mr. McCluskie. What can we do for you? Hope that room met with your satisfaction. We don't often get folks like yourself in here. Railroad men, I mean. Mostly the rougher crowd. Y'know, trailhands and muleskinners and the like."

McCluskie simply ignored the chatter. He took out the makings and started building a smoke. "Need some directions. Belle Siddons' house on Third Street."

The clerk's smile widened into a sly, dirty grin. "You sure know how to pick 'em, Mr. McCluskie. Belle's got the best sportin' house in town. Oughta warn you, though, it's awful expensive."

McCluskie nailed him with a flat, dull stare. "Something tickle your funny bone?"

The man blinked a couple of times and looked a little closer. What he saw was a face that sobered anyone with the savvy to read it. His grin dissolved into a waxen smile.

"No offense, Mr. McCluskie. Just tryin' to be friendly. Service of the house."

"Forget it. What about the directions?"

"Sure thing. Belle's house is just this side of Hide

Park. Big yellow house right on the corner of Third. You won't have no trouble recognizing it."

"What's Hide Park?"

"Why, the—uh—y'know. The sportin' district. The parlor houses are on Third and down below that are the dancehalls and the cribs. That's why they call it Hide Park. Nothin' but bare skin and lots of it."

McCluskie just stared at him for a moment, then turned and walked from the hotel.

Striding down South Main, the Irishman found it about as he had expected. Within the first block there was a grocery, two hotels, a mercantile, and a hardware store. Then for the next couple of blocks both sides of the street were lined with saloons and gambling dens. Evidently everything below that was Hide Park.

The more he saw, the better he liked it. Plainly the townspeople had been at some pains to lay it out properly. Newton straddled the Chisholm Trail and was sixty-five miles south of Abilene. Which meant that its future as a cowtown was pretty well assured. At least for a couple of seasons, anyway. Once track was laid into Wichita, some twenty miles farther south, Newton's bubble would burst like a dead toad in a hot sun. But that was for him to know and them to find out. There was nothing to be gained in letting it get around that the Santa Fe had a finger in the pie. Right now it was enough to wean the Texans away from Abilene. The next step would come in its own good time.

Late afternoon shadows splayed over the town, and already the street was crowded with Texans. Watching them as he strolled along, McCluskie marveled again at the cowhands' childlike antics. Somehow they never seemed to change. After two months on the trail, eating dust and beans and working themselves to a frazzle, they couldn't wait to scatter their money to the winds. Painted women, watered-down whiskey, and rigged card games. That was about their speed. Almost as if they had some perverse craving to be flimflammed out of the dollar a day they earned wet-nursing longhorns. It just went to prove what most sensible folks already knew. Texans, give or take a handful, weren't much brighter than the cows they drove to railhead.

Still, a man had to give the devil his due. Without the Texans and their longhorns, the Santa Fe would be hard pushed to pull off the scheme that brought him to Newton. The thought triggered another, and he reminded himself to have a look at North Main before dark. Might even be well to introduce himself to some of the town fathers. Let them know he was around if they needed a hand with anything. Texans or otherwise. Never hurt to have a foot in the door with the uptown crowd. Especially the ones who fancied themselves as politicians.

Nearing Third, he spotted the yellow house on the northeast corner and angled across the street. Inspecting it closer, he decided the room clerk had been right after all. Upside the drab buildings surrounding it, the yellow house stuck out like a diamond in an ash heap.

McCluskie went through the door without bothering to knock and found himself in a small vestibule. The layout was as familiar as an old shoe and he proceeded immediately to the parlor. There he came on a black maid, humming softly to herself as she set things in order for the evening rush. She straightened up and gave him a toothy smile.

"Mistah, you're gonna hafta come back. I knows you got the misery jest from lookin' at you, but we ain't open till aftah suppahtime."

That was something he had always admired about Belle. She taught the help how to diddle a man and make him like it. Even maids.

"Tell Miss Belle she's got a gentleman caller."

Apparently that was a new one on the black woman. Her sloe eyes batted furiously for a moment, then she hitched around and scurried from the room. As she went through a door to the back part of the house, she muttered something unintelligible. From the little he could make out, it was a fairly one-sided conversation.

Left to himself, McCluskie examined the parlor with a critical eye. It was nothing less than he would have expected of Belle Siddons. She had a reputation for running an elegant house. Not at all like the two-bit cribs and dollar-a-dance palaces down the street. Plainly, from the looks of the parlor, she hadn't lost her touch. Grunting, he silently gave the room his stamp of approval.

"Well as I live and breathe! If it's not the big Mick himself."

Turning, he saw Belle standing in the doorway, smiling that same soft smile he remembered so well. Outwardly she seemed to have changed not at all, though it was something over a year since he had last seen her.

She wasn't a small woman, yet there was a delicacy to her that somehow belied the shapely hips and full bust. Her hair was the color of a raven's wing, glinted through with specks of rust when the light struck it just right, and her eyes had always reminded him of an emerald stickpin he once saw on a riverboat gambler. But it was her face that stopped most men. Not hard or worn, like what a fellow who frequented sporting houses would expect to find on a madam. It was an easy face to look at, pleasurable. Maybe something short of beautiful, but with a devilish witchery that made a man sit up and do tricks just so he could watch it smile.

"Belle, you look nifty as ever." McCluskie was hard put to keep from licking his mustache. "Appears life's been treatin' you with style."

"I can't complain." She walked toward him, airily waving her hand around the parlor. "What's the verdict? Think it'll pass muster?"

McCluskie caught a whiff of jasmine scent as she stopped before him, and for a moment he couldn't get his tongue untracked. "The house? Why, sure. Even classier than the place you had in Abilene."

"Yes, good old Abilene. Every now and then I think back on it and have myself a real laugh." A curious light flickered in her eyes. Somehow it put him in mind of a tiny flame bouncing off of alabaster. "But that's water under the bridge. Tell me about yourself, Mike. What have you been doing since the good old days?"

The way she was looking at him made him uncomfortable as hell. Almost as if he should be scuffling his toe in the dirt and apologizing for some fool thing he'd done.

"Nothin' much. Just pickin' up a dollar here and a dollar there."

"I do declare, a modest Irishman. Never thought I'd live to see the day."

"Well, you know me, Belle. I never was one to toot my own horn."

"Don't be bashful, honey. You're among friends. Why, everybody in Kansas has heard about Mike McCluskie. Some folks say the Santa Fe would fall apart without him to fend off those big, bad train robbers."

The conversation wasn't going quite the way McCluskie had expected. In fact, it seemed to be all uphill, with him pulling the load. He decided to try another tack.

"I just got in this afternoon. Thought I'd come down and invite you out for a bite to eat after you close up tonight."

"Then we could go up to your room for a drink and talk about old times."

McCluskie grinned. "Well, something like that had crossed my mind."

Fire flashed in Belle's eyes, and it was no longer a tiny flame. "Listen you thick-headed Mick, forget the sweet talk and trot yourself out of here. You left me high and dry in Abilene, and once burned is twice beware. So just scoot!"

"Aw, hell, Belle. It wasn't like—"

"Don't 'aw, Belle' me, you big baboon! Waltz on down the street and find yourself another sucker. They're a dime a dozen and standing in line."

Singed around the ears and smoking hot, he headed for the vestibule. "Well, don't say I never asked you.

If you change your mind I'm stayin' at the National."

"Don't hold your breath," she fired back. "And don't let the door hit you in the keester on the way out!"

McCluskie didn't. But he came near jarring it off the hinges when it slammed shut behind him.

TWO

McCluskie stalked back up Main Street like a mad bull hooking at cobwebs. With each step his temper flared higher and his mood turned darker. There was just no rhyme nor reason to Belle's attitude. There'd never been any understanding between them, and she sure as hell hadn't had any claim on him. She'd known that from the outset when they started keeping company back in Abilene. It was simply an arrangement. Pleasant enough, and something they had both seemed to need at the time. But nothing more. Just two people having a few laughs and enjoying one another whenever the mood struck them.

That was the trouble with women. They could never accept a little monkey business for what it was. Somehow it always came out larded with mush and lickety-split got itself embroidered into a four letter word. L-O-V-E. Even crib girls weren't immune to the disease. Countless times he'd seen blowsy tarts go sweet on a certain man and just eat their hearts out when they couldn't have him all to themselves. While all the time they were plying their trade regular as clockwork.

It surpassed all understanding. Goddamn if it didn't!

Yet, when it got down to brass tacks, that wasn't what had him boiling. Lots of females had got that goofy look after he'd flushed the birds out of their nest. That was something a fellow learned to live with, for it seemed to be the universal affliction of anything that wore skirts. What had his goat—and the mere thought of it set him off in a rage—was that he'd never before been dusted off by a woman.

And a madam to boot!

The gall of the woman, and her not even Irish. If her name was Adair or Murphy or O'Toole, just maybe he could have swallowed it. Understood, anyway. But for the likes of Belle Siddons to think that she had something special! Something he wanted badly enough to let her put a ring through his nose.

Great crucified Christ! It defied belief.

The hell of it was, he'd never given her any reason to think that way. Not the slightest inkling. He'd always been aboveboard, a square shooter from start to finish. Maybe he hadn't discouraged her. Or put the quietus on her syrupy talk. But that was no reason for her to give him frostbite now. Merely because he'd pulled up stakes in Abilene without inviting her along. There just wasn't room for a woman in his line of work. Not a regular woman anyway. Belle had been around long enough to know that. Leastways if she hadn't then she must have had her head stuck in the sand.

Yet she had still kicked his butt out the door!

McCluskie was barreling along under a full head of steam when the doors of the Red Front Saloon suddenly burst open and he collided head on with a half dozen Texans. One look told him that they were pretty well ossified, and mad as he was, he started to let it pass. Just at the moment he figured he had all the troubles he could say grace over. Besides which, there was nothing to be gained in swapping insults with a bunch of trailhands. Shouldering them aside, he plowed through and headed up the street.

"Jes a goddamn minute, friend! Who'ya think yer shovin' around?"

The big talker knew he had made a mistake when the pilgrim in the bowler hat wheeled about and started back. McCluskie was obviously no friend. The Texan wasn't so drunk that he couldn't recognize a grizzly bear when he saw one, and he had the sinking sensation that he was on the verge of becoming somebody's supper. Out of sheer reflex he made a grab for his gun, but he never had a chance.

McCluskie's fist caught him flush on the jaw and he went down like a sack of mud. The suddenness of it was a little too much for the other cowhands. They just stood there slack-jawed and bewildered, gawking at their poleaxed comrade as if he had been struck by lightning.

The Irishman rubbed his knuckles and glowered down on them. "Anybody care to be next?"

Apparently it wasn't a thought that merited deep consideration. Even at five to one the Texans weren't wild about the odds. Not after the way their partner had nearly got his head torn off. They just shook their heads, exchanging sheepish glances, and let it slide.

McCluskie spun on his heel and walked off, just the least bit irked with himself. He shouldn't have let a loudmouth drunk set him off that way. Anger was something to be conserved, held back, so that a man could choose his own time and place to let fly. Otherwise he'd get snookered into fighting on somebody else's terms, which was a damn fine way to wind up with a busted skull.

Still, he wasn't fooling himself on where the score stood. It was Belle that had set him off. Not the Texans. If anything, the cowhand was just an innocent bystander. And any time a woman got a man to acting like a buzz saw it was time to pull back and check the bets.

Satisfied with his estimate of the whole affair, he struck off in search of the big nabobs uptown. It was high time he quit horsing around and got down to business. Which didn't include yellow cathouses or dagger-tongued madams.

Some twenty minutes later McCluskie wandered into the Lone Star Saloon just north of the tracks. After a stop at the depot, and a brief conversation with Hansberry, he came away with an interesting piece of information. Bob Spivey, owner of the Lone Star and Newton's guiding light, was chairman of the town board. All things considered, it seemed a good place to start.

The barkeep was an amiable sort by the name of Mulhaney, who had a weakness for fellow Irishmen. Before McCluskie had time to polish off his first drink Bob Spivey had been summoned from the back room. Mulhaney positively glowed that his countryman was decked out like a Philadelphia lawyer, and made the introductions as if he were presenting a long lost cousin from the old sod. After filling their glasses, still beaming from ear to ear, the barkeep drifted off to let them get better acquainted.

Spivey hoisted his glass in salute and downed the shot in one neat gulp. Plainly he liked his own whiskey. "Welcome to Newton, Mr. McCluskie. Pardon me for sayin' it, but I can't help admirin' that suit you're wearin'. Real nice duds. Just between you and me and the gatepost, we haven't had many visitors with any real class as yet. Hope you'll decide to stay with us for a while."

"Might take you up on that." McCluskie smiled and tapped the brim of his bowler. "Don't pay any mind to this, though. It's my travelin' outfit. Once I change into workin' clothes you couldn't pick me out in a crowd."

"Is that a fact?" Spivey refilled their glasses, glancing sideways as he set the bottle on the bar. "If you don't mind my askin', what line of work are you in?"

The question was breach of etiquette in a cowtown, and both men knew it. But Spivey was playing the role of a well-meaning, if somewhat curious, host. His face bore the look of a plaster saint, all innocence.

McCluskie didn't bat an eye. "I'm with the railroad. The Santa Fe."

"Well now, that is news." Spivey's grin suddenly turned spare, inquiring. "Would I be out of line in askin' what brings you to our fair metropolis?"

"Nope, not at all. Understand you folks are gettin' ready to open a bank."

"That a fact. The Cattlemen's Exchange. You

might have noticed it directly across the street. But I don't see the connection, just exactly."

"The money shipment will be comin' in on tomorrow evening's train. I sort of look after things like that for the Santa Fe."

"I see." The saloonkeeper's gaze drifted off a moment, then snapped back. "Say, wait a minute. McCluskie? Aren't you the fellow that used to ride shotgun for the K&P up in Abilene?"

"Yeah, I did a turn or two along the Smoky Hill."

"Then you're the one that killed the Quinton brothers when they tried to hold up that express car."

"Guess you got me pegged, all right. Course, that was about a hundred lifetimes ago."

"Well I'll be dipped. Mike McCluskie." Spivey's mouth widened in a toothsome grin. "Hell, I feel safer about our money already. I'm just guessin', but I'd speculate the Santa Fe sent you out here to see that things come off without a hitch."

"That's close enough, I guess." McCluskie paused, knuckling back his mustache, and decided on the spur of the moment that it was time to test the water. "Newt Hansberry tells me you're the he-wolf on the town board. Thought we might have a little talk about this lawman of yours. I'm sort of curious as to how much help he'll be if push comes to shove."

"You mean if somebody tries to rob the train?" When the Irishman nodded, Spivey gave him a concerned look. "That sounds like you know something we don't."

"Wouldn't say that exactly. But when you're talkin' about that much money it never hurts to hedge your bet."

"Then you know the amount being shipped?" McCluskie just stared at him, saying nothing. "Listen, if there's anything in the wind, I'd like to hear about it. Just between you and me, I own a piece of that bank, and all this talk of train robbers don't do my nerves much good."

"Mr. Spivey, I knew you were in on the bank deal before I came out here. Otherwise I wouldn't even be talkin' to you. But so far as I've been able to find out, there's nobody plannin' a stick up. Like I said, I just wanted the lowdown on this deputy of yours. In case I had to call on him."

"Well there's not a whole lot I can tell you. He's from Wichita, y'see. The county sent him up here after a bunch of us pitched in and raised a kitty to pay his salary. Way we figured it, the town needed some sort of John Law to keep the Texans in line. So far Hazeltine's done the job. Leastways we haven't had no killin's."

"Has anybody braced him yet?"

"Can't say as they have. He don't believe in postin' a gun ordinance. Says it can't be enforced without a lot of killin'. So far nobody's tried him on for size, if that's what you mean."

"Something like that."

"Guess I can't help you there. All we know is that he's supposed to be some kind o' tough nut. The sheriff says he's a real stemwinder. Evidently made himself a reputation somewheres down in the Nations. Tell you the truth, though, you sort of lost me. What's Hazeltine got to do with a Santa Fe money shipment? I always heard you boys weren't exactly slouches at lookin' after your own business."

"We generally manage." McCluskie's look revealed nothing. "But it don't hurt to take a peek at your hole card, just in case you have to play it. Might be an ace and it might be a joker. Pays to know what you're holdin'."

Spivey fell silent, sipping at his whiskey. He was a short man, tending to bald with the years, and he perspired a lot. Mainly from the bulge around his beltline, which was the result of indulging himself with good food and plentiful liquor. But what he lacked in size and muscle he made up for with an agile, inquiring mind. In the past he had been able to stay a step ahead of bigger men simply by outwitting them, and it was this ferret-like shrewdness which had given him some degree of influence in the affairs of Newton. Right now that inquisitive nature was focused on the Irishman. Something about McCluskie's sudden appearance and his guileless manner just didn't jell. Granted, the money shipment warranted the presence of someone of McCluskie's caliber, but there was something here that didn't meet the eye. Puzzling over it, he decided to try a shot in the dark.

"Say, I just remembered something I wanted to ask you about. You being a railroad man and all." Spivey's expression was bland but watchful, searching for any telltale sign. "What's the word at Santa Fe about this new outfit down in Wichita? Way I heard it, a couple of sharp operators name of Meade and Grieffenstein are tryin' to promote themselves a railroad."

McCluskie didn't even blink. "Beats me. There's so many small-timers around a man's hard put to keep 'em sorted out. Why, they been up here tryin' to dump some stock?"

"Naw, they're smarter'n that." The saloonkeeper hadn't detected anything suspicious, but he wasn't willing to let it drop so easily. "They're tryin' to float a bond issue by organizin' a referendum vote. Course, they got the courthouse crowd in their hip pockets, but that don't go for all of Sedgwick County. Up here, we mean to fight 'em right down to the wire."

"That so? Any special reason?"

"Reason? Why, hell yes! You mean to say you don't know where they intend to build this railroad?"

"Don't recollect hearin' one way or the other."

"That curious, for a fact, since they mean to run a line between Wichita and here. Offhand I'd think the Santa Fe wouldn't let a piece of news like that slip past 'em. Naturally, you can see that if the bond issue ever went through, Newton'd be dead as a doornail. Leastways where the cattle trade is concerned."

Whatever reaction this sparked in the Irishman, Spivey missed it completely. His little game came to an abrupt end as the door burst open and a man stomped in as if he was looking for a dog to kick. The cast of his eye said that it didn't make much difference which dog. Just any that happened to be handy would do nicely.

McCluskie caught the glint of a badge and his interest perked up. The man striding toward them was tall and slim, and there was something glacial about his face. Almost as if it had been shrunk and frozen and nailed down tight, so that nothing moved but his eyes. Nature hadn't let him off that lightly, though. His teeth were stained and square as cubes, not unlike a row of old dice, and his eyes gave off a peculiar glassy sparkle. Queer as it seemed, he looked like a stuffed eagle that had had a couple of marbles wedged into his eye sockets.

Plainly, this was Tonk Hazeltine. Newton's principal claim to law and order.

The deputy marched up to Spivey and gave him a hard as nails scowl. "You heard about it?"

"About what?" Spivey sounded like a befuddled parrot.

"Don't nobody in this town keep their ears open 'cept me?" Hazeltine's curt tone was underscored by a kind of smothered wrath. "Some jasper just cold-cocked a drover down at the Red Front and the lid like t' blew off. I hadda hell of a time talkin' them boys out o' startin' a war. Got it in their heads they was gonna tree the whole shebang 'til they found this bird and hauled his ashes."

"Well, Tonk, that don't sound like a major calamity to me. I mean, it was just a fight, wasn't it?"

"Fight, hell! The way them boys tell the story, it was closer to murder. This feller stiffed him with one punch and come near cripplin' him for life. Why, the boy only woke up a minute ago. He's still stumblin' around like a blind dog in a slaughterhouse."

"Then why don't you just arrest this rowdy for disturbin' the peace? Seems to me that'd be the simplest way 'round the whole thing."

"Can't find him, that's why. Searched all over town and ain't seen hide nor hair of him. Them boys said he was about seven feet tall, with a big bushy mustache, and sportin' one of them hats like the drummers—"

Something clicked in Hazeltine's head and his eyes glistened like soapy agates. Since storming into the saloon he hadn't paused for wind, and in a sudden rush of awareness, he finally swiveled around for a look at the Irishman.

McCluskie grinned. "Deputy, it appears you've got your man."

"Well I'll be go to hell." Hazeltine's jaw snapped shut in a grim line. "Mister, you're under—"

Spivey broke in hurriedly. "Now hold on a minute, Tonk. This here's Mike McCluskie. Chief security agent for the Santa Fe. You can't go arrestin' him for clobberin' some damn trailhand."

"Who says I can't? 'Sides, I already told you, it weren't no fistfight. It was a massacre. Why, he's likely addled that boy permanent."

Spivey groaned and shot the Irishman an imploring look. "What about it, McCluskie? You must've had some reason to hit that drover."

"Best reason I know of. He tried pullin' a gun on me."

"The hell you say!" Hazeltine's lip curled back over his yellow teeth. "That whole bunch is ready to swear you jumped that boy before he even had time to get unlimbered."

"What you're sayin' is that one of them let the cat out of the bag about him makin' a grab for his gun."

"Is that right, Tonk?" Spivey demanded.

"What if it is? He just reached. Never even cleared leather."

The saloonkeeper let out a long sigh. "What d'ya say we just forget it? Seems pretty clear that Mr.

McCluskie was provoked and I got an idea the judge would see it the same way."

Hazeltine glowered back at him for a moment, then turned his gaze on the Irishman. "Mister, you'd better watch that stuff in my town. Next time it won't go so easy. Railroad or no railroad."

McCluskie regarded him with impassive curiosity. "Heard you made quite a name for yourself down in the Nations."

"What's that to you?"

"Nothin'. Just funny, that's all. Way I heard it, the tribes don't allow a white man to wear a badge down there."

Hazeltine tried staring him down and found that he couldn't. At last, face mottled with anger, he brushed past and stalked out of the saloon. McCluskie watched him through the door, then grunted, looking back at Spivey.

"Just offhand I'd say that's the queerest lookin' breed I ever saw."

"Breed? Why hell, McCluskie, he's got no more Injun blood in him than you do."

"Think not?" McCluskie idly toyed with his glass, joining a chain of wet little rings on the bar.

"Well, maybe you're right. Course, that being the case, I'd give a bunch to know which side he was ridin' with when he made that name for himself."

"What d'ya mean, which side?"

"Why, there's only two sides, Mr. Spivey. Always has been. And one of 'em don't wear badges."

The saloonkeeper started to say something, but couldn't quite manage to get it out. McCluskie filled their glasses again and lifted his own in salute.

"Here's mud in your eye."

THREE

The sun was an orange ball of fire, settling slowly earthward, when McCluskie came out of the cafe. He paused for a moment, working at his teeth with a toothpick, and speculated on the evening ahead. The train wasn't due in for a couple of hours, which left him with time on his hands and damn few ways to spend it. Wine, women, or cards. That's about what it boiled down to in a whistlestop like Newton. Texans had little use for much else, and the vultures who preyed on them were old hands at keeping the entertainment raw and uncomplicated.

Mulling it over, he decided that women were out. Leastways for tonight, anyway. He still hadn't simmered down from yesterday's donnybrook with Belle, and it bothered him more than he cared to admit. Oddly enough, her raking him over the coals that way had made him want her all the more. There was something about a woman with spirit that made the game a little spicier, and there was no denying that Belle could be a regular spitfire when the notion struck her.

Trouble was, she could get awful damned possessive in the bargain. Which sort of threw cold water on the whole deal.

Still the idea of stopping off at one of the other houses left a sour taste in his mouth. Maybe tomorrow, or the next day, after he'd got Belle off his mind. It wasn't like he had to have a woman, anyhow. There were lots of things a man needed worse, although at the moment nothing occurred to him that just exactly fitted the ticket.

Grunting, he snapped the toothpick in half and flipped it into the street. Hell, it was too damned hot to start messing around anyway. That was one thing a man could always count on. Kansas in July. Hotter'n Hades, and not enough shade to cool a midget.

They ought to give it back to the Indians.

With women crossed off his list, that left only cards and whiskey. McCluskie hauled out the makings and started building a smoke. Dusk wasn't far off, and what with the money shipment set to arrive, he didn't rightly have time to get himself snarled up in a poker game. A man needed to be loose and easy when he gambled, with nothing on his mind but the fickle lady. Otherwise some slick operator would punch his ticket and hand him his head on a platter.

Besides, Santa Fe trains had been known to come in on time. Not often, and certainly with nothing that would tempt a man to set his watch by their regularity. But every now and then an engineer somehow managed to limp into a station at the appointed hour. In a way, it was sort of like bucking the roulette wheel. Pick a number and make your bet. There was a winner every time and no such thing as a sure-fire cinch. Which went double for the Santa Fe. The odds went out the window where their train schedules were concerned.

By process of elimination, McCluskie had pretty well whittled down his alternatives. Women and cards would have to wait, and in Newton that made for slim pickings. Whiskey seemed to be the only thing left, and the way things were shaping up, a pair of wet tonsils sounded better all the time. Little gargle water might just do wonders for his mood.

Flicking a match, he lit his cigarette and headed toward the tracks. He could just as easily have crossed the street and had a drink at the Lone Star. But tonight he didn't feel like matching wits with Spivey. It was a dull pastime anyhow. The saloonkeeper was sharp as a tack in his own way, but he was about as subtle as a sledgehammer. Thought he was going to outfox the big dumb Mick, and all he did was wind up getting himself sandbagged. If it wasn't so pitiful, it might have been funny. Besides, Spivey would likely turn up at the depot later anyway, so there was no sense wasting good drinking time playing cat and mouse.

South of the tracks was more McCluskie's style at any rate. Everybody down there was crooked as a dog's hind leg and nobody tried to pretend otherwise. In a queer sort of way, it was perhaps the purest form of honesty.

Crossing the tracks, it occurred to the Irishman that he tended to think of them as birds of prey. Most were just vultures. Hovering around, waiting to pick the bones after the trailhands had been shorn of their illusions and their pocketbooks. In this class could be lumped together the soiled doves and dancehall operators and saloonkeepers. Of course, there were the turkey buzzards, too. Like Rowdy Joe Lowe and his wife, Crazy Kate. They were the real carrion eaters, the bottom of the heap. What they wouldn't do for a nickel hadn't yet been invented.

Looking at it the other way round, though, the sporting crowd had its own brand of nobility. At the top were the hawks, and a mere handful of crafty old owls. This group, small in number and worlds apart from the grungy bone-pickers, was comprised strictly of highrollers, bunco artists, thimble riggers, and slippery fingered gamblers. Not a tinhorn among them. The elite of whatever underworld they chose to frequent.

Already McCluskie had heard that the highrollers were flocking to Newton like a gathering of royalty. Dandy John Gallagher. Jim Moon. Pony Reid. Names to be reckoned with wherever men talked of faro, three-card monte, chuck-a-luck, or poker. Beside them the likes of Ben Thompson and Bill Hickok and Phil Coe were small potatoes. Amateurs. Chickenfeed sparrows trying to fly high in the company of hawks.

Passing Hoff's Grocery, he noted that the southside was already humming. Cow ponies lined the hitch rails, standing hipshot and drowsy in the dusky heat. Their owners, either three sheets to the wind or fast on their way, were in evidence everywhere along the street. After nearly two years in Abilene, McCluskie could just about slot Texans into the right pigeonhole simply by observing their actions.

The newcomers, fresh off the trail, made a beeline for some place like the Blue Front Clothing Store, splurging a hefty chunk of their pay on fancy duds. Those who had had a bath and sprinkled themselves with toilet water could be found in one of three places. Getting their ears unwaxed down in Hide Park. Swilling snakehead whiskey at two-bits a throw. Or testing their none-too-nimble wits against the slick-fingered cardsharps. The ones who gave lessons in instant poverty.

Lastly, there was the motley crew who were flat on their rumps. Broke, busted, and hungover. Most times they could be spotted cadging drinks, or loafing around Hamil's Hardware eyeballing Sam Colt's latest equalizer. Some of these were reduced to selling their saddles in order to get home, which in a Texan's scheme of things was only slightly less heinous than herding sheep.

McCluskie had to laugh everytime he thought about it. Whichever way a man looked at it, cowhands were a queer breed. They had the brass of a billygoat, but the Good Lord had somehow put their behinds where their brains were supposed to be. Heaven for them didn't have nothing to do with the Hereafter. It was fast women and a jug of rotgut. In just that order.

Shouldering past a bunch of drunks crowding the boardwalk, he pushed through the doors of the Gold Room Saloon. The Texans paid him no mind this time. He was garbed in a linsey shirt, mule-ear boots, and a slouch hat. Along with the Colt Navy strapped high on his hip, the outfit made him one of the crowd. Taller than most, beefier through the shoulders perhaps, but to all appearances just another sporting man out to see the elephant. Which was exactly how he liked it. Having worked his way up from a track layer, he always felt more at ease among men who sweated for a living. Even Texans.

Apparently the Gold Room was one of Newton's better watering holes. Unlike most of the dives, it wasn't jammed to the rafters with caterwauling trail-hands. Then he saw the reason. Standing at the bar was Dandy John Gallagher. High priest of the gambling fraternity.

Plainly he had stumbled upon the lair of the high-rollers. Where sparrows and pigeons alike were separated from their pokes with style and consummate skill.

Walking forward, he stopped at Gallagher's elbow, who was in the midst of lecturing another man on the merits of some strange new game called Red Dog.

"Mister, I'm lookin' fer a tinhorn name o' Gallagher. The one they run out o' Abilene fer dealin' seconds."

The gambler went stiff as a board, shoulders squared, and slowly turned around. The look in his eye would have melted a cannonball. Then, quite suddenly, the tight-lipped scowl exploded into an infectious grin.

"Mike! You sorry devil. Put'er there!"

McCluskie clasped his hand in a hard grip. "Been a long time, Johnny."

"Too long, by God." Gallagher gave a final shake, then jerked a thumb at his companion. "Why, not ten minutes ago I was saying to Trick here—hey, you two haven't met. Mike McCluskie, say hello to Trick Brown."

The two men hardly had time to exchange nods before Gallagher was off again. "Anyways, I was saying to Trick that there just aren't enough real gambling men around these days. No competition. But, hell's bells, now that you're here, I might just change my tune."

"Johnny, you're out of my league. No contest."

"Don't grease me, boy. I've seen you play. Remember?"

"Hell, I ought to. The lessons cost me enough."

"Judas Priest! You could churn that stuff and make apple butter. C'mon now, Mike, what do you say? Let's get a real headknocker going. Table stakes. Straight stud. Just like the old days."

"Well, I guess I might try you on for size. Just for old time's sake, you understand. But it'll have to be later tonight. I've got an errand to tend to first."

The gambler punched him on the shoulder. "Something young and full of ginger, I'll lay odds. Never change, do you?"

McCluskie laughed easily. "You've got a lot of room to talk. I didn't feel any calluses on your hand. Bet you're still coatin' them with glycerin morning, noon, and night, aren't you?"

"Christ A'mighty, Irish! They're tools of the trade. Wouldn't want me to disgrace the profession, would you?"

McCluskie was distracted by someone waving from a faro layout at the back of the room. He looked closer and saw that it was Pony Reid. "Listen, I'm gonna have a quick drink and say hello to Pony. I'll catch up with you somewhere around midnight. Just don't let anybody peel your roll till I get back."

"Fat chance. Take care you don't get waylaid yourself. Remember, Irish, a poker game is elixir for the soul. You keep that in mind, you hear?"

McCluskie was still laughing as he strode toward Pony Reid. Gallagher and Brown watched after him a moment, then turned back to their drinks. Brown sipped at his liquor for a minute, apparently lost in thought, and finally glanced over at his friend.

"Johnny, did I get the drift right? The way you talked that hayseed is some kind of bearcat with a deck of cards."

"He's more than that, Trick. In a straight game he could hold his own with anyone you want to name."

"Yeah? Well I'll bet I've got a few moves that'll leave him cross-eyed. Maybe I ought to sit in on that game myself. We might just clean his plow faster'n scat."

Gallagher seemed vastly amused by the idea. "Trick, you're new to the circuit, so I'm going to give you some free advice. Don't ever try to slick Mike McCluskie. He'll kill you quicker than anthrax juice. Looks are deceiving, my boy, and if you're going to live long in this trade, you'd better learn to size a man up. What you just saw wasn't a hayseed. It's a Bengal tiger crossed with an Irish wolfhound."

The gambler's pale, milky eyes drifted again toward the back of the room. "Besides, he could probably outdeal you with his thumbs chopped off."

McCluskie left the Gold Room an hour or so later. His humor was restored and his mood was considerably lighter. While he'd meant to have only one drink, he found it difficult to quit the genial company. There was a camaraderie among professional gamblers that had always intrigued him, and strangely enough, he felt drawn to it in a way he had never fully fathomed. Not that he was blinded to their flaws. They had feet of clay just like everyone else, and the brotherhood they shared was dictated more by circumstances than any need of fellowship. Essentially they were loners, preying on the unwary and the gullible with no more scruples than an alleycat. Within the fraternity there were petty squabbles and jealousies, and an incessant bickering as to who held title to King of the Hill. The same as would be found among any group of men who lived by their wits and felt themselves superior to the great unwashed herd.

Yet there was a solidarity among gamblers that was rare in men of any stripe. They saw themselves as a small band of gallants pitted against the whole world. Though each of them was concerned with feathering his own nest, they could close ranks in an instant when it suited their purpose. Such as combining forces to trim a well-heeled sucker, or standing together when confronted by an indignant mob of righteous townspeople. More than that, they seemed to genuinely enjoy each other's company, much as a breed apart prefers its own kind, and their good-natured banter was seldom extended to outsiders. Except for a select few who were somehow allowed to join the inner circle.

McCluskie was one of those. A fellow lone wolf. The fact that he played shrewd poker, and on occasion had sent even the best of them back to the well, was only incidental. They accepted him mainly because, when it got right down to the nub, he shared their outlook on life. The Irishman didn't give a damn for the entire human race, and within a congregation of cynics that made him a kindred spirit.

The offshoot of this mutual affinity was that McCluskie could meet them head-on across a gaming table without fear of being greased. With a morality peculiar to the breed, they never cheated friends. Unless, of course, it tickled their fancy. For just as they were addicted to gambling, so were they congenital scamps. With them the practical joke was a universal pastime, engineered and executed with such flair that it frequently approached an art form. Like the time Pony Reid had palmed a cold deck into the game and dealt each of the players four aces. The betting skyrocketed like a roman candle, and when it was over every man at the table had raised clean down to his stickpin and pocket watch. The showdown had been nothing short of spectacular, and the look on the players' faces was a classic study in slack-jawed stupefaction. Even years afterward, it was generally conceded that Pony Reid had taken the brass ring for sheer gall. To cold deck a gathering of one's own confederates was considered the ultimate in technical virtuosity.

McCluskie had prompted Reid to retell the yarn again tonight, when they were on their fourth drink. Now, walking up Main toward the train station, he was still chuckling to himself. Taken as a whole, gamblers were a cutthroat bunch. Born thieves with no more conscience than a hungry spider. But they were likeable rogues, practicing their own brand of honor, and in a curious way, a notch above those who used the law to whitewash their sleazy schemes. Leastways it had always been his observation that not all of a town's rascals came from the wrong side of the tracks.

Mounting the steps to the depot platform, McCluskie's amiable mood did a bellyflop. Standing there, like a double dose of ice water, was Newt Hansberry and his assistant flunky, Ringbone Smith.

"Evenin', Mike."

"Evenin', Newt."

"Howdy do, Mr. McCluskie."

McCluskie just nodded to Smith. They had met earlier in the day and Smith impressed him as a near miss of some sort. A gangling lout whose name was derived from his habit of wearing a hollowed-out marrow bone on his pinky finger. Seeing them together, the Irishman felt his good cheer begin to curdle. A long-nosed busybody and a dimdot who had been shortchanged when the marbles were passed out.

It was a match made in heaven.

Hansberry hawked and spat a wad of phlegm at the tracks. "Gettin' on time for that train of yours. Oughta be seein' it any minute now."

McCluskie eyed him narrowly. "Had any word from up the line?"

"Nope, nary a peep. Seems like ever'body's got lockjaw where that train of yours is concerned."

"Newt, I'm not interested one way or the other especially, but what makes you think that it's *my* train?"

"Well, it ain't like it's a regular run, now is it! I mean, hell's fire and little fishes. I didn't even know the dangblasted thing was comin' in till you told me this mornin'."

"The Santa Fe moves in mysterious ways, Newt. Not that it performs many wonders."

"*Humph!*" Hansberry snorted and screwed his face up in a walleyed look of righteous indignation. "Y'know, I am the station master around here. Seems like some people has a way of forgettin' that."

"You're thinkin' the brass should've informed you official-like. Instead of leavin' it to me."

"That'd do for openers. Contrary to what some folks think, I ain't the head mop jockey around here. I run this place with a pretty tight hand, and seems to me I oughta know what's what and whyfor."

"Guess it all depends on how you look at it. Some things are for the doing and not the talking. What you don't know can't hurt you. Specially if you keep your trap shut."

McCluskie saw Spivey and Tonk Hazeltine approaching with a stranger. Leaving Hansberry to fry in his own fat, the Irishman walked off to meet the greeting committee. The safest bet in town was that they would have been on hand to oversee the money shipment.

Ringbone Smith whistled softly through his teeth, spraying his chin with spit. "Lordy mercy, Mr. H. That feller must've been brung up on sour milk to get so downright techy."

Hansberry just grunted, and ground his jaws in quiet fury. Sometimes he wished he were back on the farm slopping hogs. Lately he'd come to think that pigs were downright civil alongside some people he knew.

FOUR

McCluskie stopped short of the three men and waited. Leaning back against a freight cart, he started rolling a smoke. Out of the corner of his eye he saw them mount the steps, and for some reason he was reminded of an old homily that Irishmen were fond of quoting.

"The fat and the lean are never what they seem."

Spivey and the stranger were both on the stout side. The charitable word would have been portly, but McCluskie wasn't feeling charitable. They looked like a couple of blubberguts that had just put a boardinghouse out of business. One thing was for sure. Matched up against one another, the pair of them would make a hell of a race at a pie-eating contest.

Trailing behind them, Hazeltine seemed like a starved dog herding a couple of hogs. He was what Texans called a long drink of water, only more so. Standing sideways in a bright sun, his shadow wouldn't have covered a gatepost. The brace of Remingtons cross-cinched over his hips seemed likely to drag him under if he ever stepped in a mud puddle.

McCluskie stuck the cigarette in his mouth and lit it, purposely letting them come to him. It was an old trick, but effective. Forcing the other man to make the first move, especially with talk and shaking hands. Somehow it put them on the defensive, just the least bit off balance. Considering the unlikely trio bearing down on him, it was a dodge well suited to the moment.

Spivey commenced grinning the minute he cleared the steps. "Mike, where the hell you been all day? Thought sure you'd drop by for a drink."

McCluskie exhaled a small cloud of smoke. "Couldn't squeeze it in. Had some business that needed tendin'."

"No doubt. No doubt." Spivey fairly oozed good cheer. "Well don't make yourself a stranger, you hear?" Suddenly his jowls dimpled in a rubbery smile. "Say, I almost forgot you two don't know each other. This here's Judge Randolph Muse, our local magistrate. Randy, shake hands with Mike McCluskie."

The Irishman waited, letting the older man extend his hand. Only then did he take it, nodding slightly. "Judge. Pleased to meet you."

Randolph Muse was no fledgling. He knew the gambit well, had used it on other men most of his life. Still, he'd let himself get sucked in. His ears burned, and despite a stiff upper lip, he felt like a bumbling ass. Perhaps Spivey was right, after all. This ham-fisted Mick would bear watching.

"The pleasure's all mine, Mr. McCluskie. Bob has been telling me about you. According to him, you're about the toughest thing to come down the pike since Wild Bill himself."

"That's layin' it on pretty thick, Judge. From what I hear, Hickok's got Abilene treed about the same way he did Hays City. Just offhand, I don't think I'd want to try twistin' a knot in his tail."

Tonk Hazeltine snorted through his nose. "Hell! Hickok ain't so much. Just got himself a reputation, that's all. There's lots of men that could dust him off 'fore he ever had time to get started."

Spivey and Muse looked embarrassed. McCluskie blew the ashes off his cigarette and studied the coal without expression. It was obvious to everyone that the lawman's raspy statement was sheer braggadocio. A penny-ante gunslick tooting his own bugle. With all the finesse of a lead mallet.

The saloonkeeper cleared his throat and nimbly changed the subject. "Mike, what time's this train suppose to be in, anyway? Near as I recollect, all you ever said was somewhere after suppertime."

McCluskie smiled and cocked one eye eastward along the tracks. "With the Santa Fe it's sorta a case of you pays your money and you takes your chances. I didn't give you an exact time because my crystal ball is busted."

"You mean to say nobody's got any idea of when it'll be in?"

"Your guess is as good as mine, I reckon. Best I can tell you is that we'll know it's here when we see it."

The judge grumped something that sounded faintly like a belch. "That's a hell of a way to run a railroad, if you don't mind my saying so."

McCluskie eyed him closer in the flickering light from the depot lantern. Clear to see, Newton's judicial wizard was a crusty old vinegaroon. Yet his character didn't exactly fit any of the handy little pigeonholes McCluskie normally used to catalogue people. There was something of a charlatan about him. Not just the precise way he spoke, or the high-falutin clothes he wore, but a secretion of some sort. A smell. The kind the Irishman had winded all too often not to recognize it when he was face to face with the live goods. All the same, he exuded a dash of dignity that lacked even the slightest trace of hokum. It was the real article. Which made for a pretty queer mixture, one that didn't lend itself to any lightning calculations. Plainly, Randolph Muse wasn't a man to be underestimated. Especially if he was tied in with Spivey somehow.

"Your Honor, I couldn't agree with you more. Course, I'm just hired help, you understand. The Santa Fe don't pay me to solve their riddles, frankly, I've never paid it much mind one way or the other. 'Fraid you'll have to take it up with the brass if you want the real lowdown."

Spivey leaped in before the judge could reply. "Now don't get off on the wrong track, Mike. Randy didn't mean nothin' personal. It's just that we've both got a lot at stake in this deal. He's one of the investors in our little bank, and it's only natural he'd be skittish about this train being late and all. Hell, to tell you the truth, I'm sorta jumpy myself. What with everyone in town knowin' we're supposed to open for business tomorrow, it kind o' puts us behind the eightball."

"I wouldn't worry too much, gents." McCluskie

took a drag off his cigarette and flipped the stub into the darkness. "The Santa Fe might be slow as molasses, but they're not in the habit of losin' strongboxes. Besides, till the money gets here, it's the railroad's lookout, not yours."

"That's all very well, Mr. McCluskie," Judge Muse remarked. "But it isn't the Santa Fe who must face the townspeople tomorrow morning if those bank doors don't open."

"Like I said, Judge. There's no need gettin' a case of the sweats. Not yet, anyway."

Spivey frowned like a constipated owl. "That's not offering us much encouragement, Mike. Just to be blunt about it, I never did understand why you're bringin' the money in at night, anyhow. Randy and me talked it over, and the way we see it, that's about the worst time you could've picked."

"It's called security. Which means doing things the way folks don't expect. Specially train robbers. So far I haven't lost any strongboxes playin' my hunches. Don't expect to lose this one either."

"Good God, man!" the judge yelped. "Are you standing there telling us that you shipped one hundred thousand dollars on a hunch?"

"Get a hunch, bet a hunch." The Irishman grinned, thoroughly amused that he'd given the two lardguts a case of the fidgets. "What you fellows can't seem to get straight is that it's out of my hands. Leastways till the train gets here."

"Judas Priest!" Spivey groaned. "That's what we're talkin' about. Where the hell is the train?"

"Somewhere between here and there, most likely. Tell you what. Why don't you and the judge go get yourselves a drink? Little whiskey never hurt anybody's nerves. When the train gets in, I'll bring your money over with a red ribbon on it."

"Don't you fret yourself none, Mr. Spivey." Tonk Hazeltine came on fast, trying to regain lost ground. "I'll stick right here and make sure ever'thing goes accordin' to snuff." He gave the holstered Remingtons a flat-handed slap. "Long as we got these backin' the play there ain't gonna be no miscues on this end."

The other men stared at him as if he had just sprouted measles. McCluskie's earlier suspicions had now been confirmed in spades. As a peace officer Tonk Hazeltine was long on luck and short on savvy. The man's attitude was that of flint in search of stone. Abrasive and needlessly pugnacious. Anybody who went around with that big chip on his shoulder was running scared. It was the act of a tinhorn trying to convince everybody he was sudden death from Bitter Creek. Inside, his guts probably quivered like jelly on a cold platter.

"Deputy, it strikes me you've pulled up a chair in the wrong game." McCluskie's voice was smooth as butter. "If I need help you'll hear me yell plenty loud. Otherwise I guess I'll just play the cards out my own way."

Hazeltine went red as ox blood, and the scorn he read in the Irishman's gaze pushed him over the edge. "Mister, you might be somethin' on a stick with your fists, but you ain't messin' around with no cowhand. I'll go wherever I goddamn please and do whatever suits me. Now if that notion ain't to your likin', whyn't you try reachin' for that peashooter on your hip."

McCluskie smiled and eased away from the freight cart. "Girls first, Tonk. You start the dance and we'll see who ends up suckin' wind."

The goad was deliberate, calculated. An insult that left a man only two outs. Fish or cut bait.

But whatever the lawman saw in McCluskie's face sent a shiver through his innards. Just for a moment he met and held the flinty gaze, then his eyes shifted away. He had a sudden premonition that the Irishman would kill him where he stood if he so much as twitched his finger.

"Another time, mebbe. When we ain't got all this money to keep watch on." Hazeltine's eyes seemed to look everywhere but at the three men. "Guess I'll mosey down and see if Newt's got any word over the wire. Wouldn't surprise me if he knows more about that train than the whole bunch of us."

The deputy walked off as if he hadn't a care in the world. But his knees somehow seemed out of joint, and when he tugged at the brim of his hat, there was a slight tremor to his hand. Spivey and Muse stared after him in pop-eyed befuddlement. They had seen it, but they couldn't quite believe it. Tonk Hazeltine with his tail between his legs. It shook them right down to the quick.

Randolph Muse was the first to recover his wits. "Mr. McCluskie, if I wasn't standing here, I'd swear on a stack of Bibles that such a thing could never happen."

"Me too," Spivey agreed. "Beats anything I ever heard tell of. Why, I would've bet every nickel I own there wasn't nothin' that could make Hazeltine eat dirt."

McCluskie started building another smoke. "Yeah, it's queer awright. The way a man'll lose his starch when his bluff gets called. Interestin' though." He licked the paper and twisted one end of the cigarette. "Seein⁻ which way it'll fall, I mean."

The older men digested that in silence and remained quiet for what seemed a long while. McCluskie's statement, perhaps more than his actions, left them momentarily nonplused. They had seen their share of hardcases since coming west. Cowtowns acted as a lodestone for the rougher element, and the sight of two men carving one another up with knives or blasting away with guns wasn't any great novelty. But they had never come across anyone exactly like the Irishman. The way he'd goaded Hazeltine was somehow inhuman, cold and calculated with a degree of fatalism that bordered on lunacy. Like a man who teases a rattler just to see if he can leap aside faster than the snake can strike. They had heard about men like that. The kind who had ice water in their veins, and through some quirk of nature, took sport in pitting themselves against danger.

McCluskie was the first one they had ever met, though, and it was a sobering experience.

Presently Judge Muse came out of his funk and remembered his purpose in being there. He tried to keep his voice casual, offhand. "Bob tells me you're chief of security for the Santa Fe."

"One handle's as good as another, I guess." McCluskie glanced at him, alerted somehow that new cards had just been dealt. "The railroad's got a habit of pastin' labels on people."

"Now that's passing strange, for a fact." Muse

stared off into the night, reflective, like a dog worrying over a bone.

The Irishman refused the bait. Leaning back against the freight cart, he puffed on his cigarette and said nothing.

After a moment, failing to get a rise out of McCluskie, the judge shook his head and grunted. The act was a good one. He looked for all the world like a man faced with a bothersome little riddle. One that stubbornly resisted a reasonable solution.

"Puzzles always intrigue me, Mr. McCluskie. Just a personal idiosyncrasy, I suppose. But something Bob said struck me as very curious. He told me that neither you nor the Santa Fe had heard about the Wichita & Southwestern."

"You mean this two-bit railroad somebody's tryin' to promote?"

"That's the one. To be more precise, the men behind it are a certain James Meade and William Grieffenstein. Reputedly, they have connections back east."

"You sort of lost me on the turn, Judge. What's a shoestring outfit like that got to do with me or the Santa Fe?"

"Well it does seem strange. That a line as large as the Santa Fe would remain in the dark on an issue this vital. Don't you agree?"

"Beats me. Course, in a way, you're talkin' to the wrong man. The Santa Fe don't tell me all its secrets, y'know. There's lots of things the brass keeps to themselves. Most likely they don't think it's as vital as you do. Assumin' they even know."

"That seems highly improbable. A line between

here and Wichita would provide some pretty stiff competition. Unless, of course, the Santa Fe bought it out."

McCluskie held back hard on a smile. The old reprobate had finally sunk the gaff. He felt Muse's bright eyes boring into him, waiting for him to squirm. It was downright pathetic. Especially from a man he'd sized up to be a slick article.

"Judge, much as I hate to admit it, all that high finance is over my head. Just offhand, though, I'd say the Santa Fe has got all the fish it can fry. What with the deadline on pushin' rails west, they're stretched pretty thin. Don't seem likely they'd start worryin' about some fleaflicker operation out of Wichita."

Spivey came to life with a sputtered oath. "By damn, there's nothin' silly about it to us! It's just like I told you, Mike. If they ever get that bond issue through, Newton's gonna dry up and blow away."

The Irishman pursed his lips and looked thoughtful. "Well, it's sort of out of my bailiwick, but if I can lend a hand some way, you give a yell. I don't guess the Santa Fe would object to me helpin' you folks out. Not with this being division point and all."

Judge Muse batted his eyes a couple of times on that and started to say something. But as his mouth opened the lonesome wail of a train whistle floated in out of the darkness. The three men looked eastward, and through the night they spotted the distant glow of an engine's headlamp. The light grew brighter as they watched, and the distinct clack of steel wheels meshing with spiked track drifted in on a light breeze. Then the train loomed up out of the darkness, passing between Hoff's Grocery and Horner's Store. A groaning squeal racketed back off the buildings as the engineer throttled down and set the brakes. Like some soot-encrusted dragon, the engine rolled past the station house and ground to a halt, belching steam and smoke and fiery sparks in a final burst of power.

Spivey and the judge stood transfixed, staring at the slat-ribbed cars in aggrieved bewilderment. It was a cattle train.

McCluskie left them open-mouthed and gawking, and walked off toward the caboose. Tonk Hazeltine, trailed by the station master and Ringbone Smith, followed along. Judge Muse and Spivey exchanged baffled frowns and joined the parade. None of them had even the vaguest notion of what was afoot, but they were determined to see the Irishman play out his string.

Climbing aboard at the forward steps, McCluskie rapped on the caboose door. There was a muffled inquiry from within and he barked a single word in response.

"McCluskie!"

The door edged open and the barrels of a sawed-off shotgun centered on his chest. Somewhere behind the cannon a disembodied voice rumbled to life.

"Everything all right out there, Mike?"

"Right as rain, Spike. Open up."

The door swung back and Spike Nugent ducked through the opening. The shotgun looked like a broomstick in his meaty paws, and the onlookers fully expected him to bound down off the train and start walking on his knuckles. He was what every young gorilla aspired to and seldom attained. Even Mc-

Cluskie seemed dwarfed by the sheer bulk of the man.

"Any trouble?" McCluskie asked.

"Quiet as a church," the burly guard observed. "Me and Jack played pinochle the whole way."

"Good. You boys get the strongbox out and we'll waltz it over to the bank. Sooner we get their receipt for it, the sooner I can get back to my poker game."

Nugent's laugh sounded like dynamite in a mountain tunnel. He turned back into the caboose and McCluskie scrambled down the steps to the station platform.

Spivey was fairly dancing with excitement. "By God, Mike, I got to hand it to you. That was slicker'n bear grease. Nobody in his right mind would've thought of lookin' in a caboose for a hundred thousand simoleons."

"That was sort of the idea," McCluskie commented.

Tonk Hazeltine stepped out from the little crowd and hitched up his crossed gunbelts. "Now that you got it here, I'll just ride herd 'tween here and the bank to make sure nobody gets any funny ideas."

McCluskie gave him a corrosive look, then shrugged. "Tag along if you want, but remember what I said. This is railroad business. You get in the way and you'll get beefed. Same as anyone else."

The lawman's reply was cut short when Spike Nugent and another man stepped through the door of the caboose. They each had a shotgun in one hand and grasped the handles of an oversized strongbox in the other. McCluskie started toward them but out of the corner of his eye he caught movement. Wheeling, he saw a shadowy figure drop from one of the forward cattle cars and take off running.

Hazeltine's arm came up with a cocked Remington, centered on the fleeing man. The impact of McCluskie's fist against his jaw gave off a mushy splat, and the deputy collapsed like a punctured accordion.

"Spike! Get that box back in the car!"

The Irishman took off in a dead sprint as the two guards lumbered back aboard the caboose. Ahead, the dim shape of a man was still visible in the flickering light from the depot lanterns. But there was something peculiar about him even in the shadowed darkness. Instead of running, he seemed to be bounding headlong in a queer, staggering lurch. Almost as if momentum alone kept him from falling. McCluskie dug harder and put on a final burst of speed.

He overtook the man just back of the engine. When he grabbed, a piece of shirt came away in his hand, and the man stumbled to a halt. McCluskie saw him turn, sensed the cocked fist, and the looping roundhouse blow. Slipping beneath the punch, the Irishman belted him in the gut and then nailed him with a left hook square on the chin. The man hit the cinders with a dusty thud and lay still.

McCluskie stooped over, gathered a handful of shirt, and began dragging the limp form toward the front of the engine. Oddly, the man didn't seem to weigh any more than a bag of wet feathers. Clearing the cowcatcher, McCluskie heaved and dumped the body in the glare of the headlamp. Then his jaws clicked shut in a wordless curse.

It was nothing but a kid. A scarecrow kid.

FIVE

McCluskie sat in a chair across the room, elbows on his knees, staring vacantly at a glass of whiskey in his hands. Every now and then he would glance up, watching the doctor for a moment, and afterward go back to studying his glass. The whiskey seemed forgotten, just something to keep his hands occupied. Whatever it was that might have distracted his mind didn't come in a bottle. Not this night, anyway.

Gass Boyd, Newton's resident sawbones, hovered around the bed like a rumpled butterfly. Though unkempt in appearance, he had a kindly bedside manner; the townspeople had found him to be a competent healer, if not a miracle worker. Since arriving in Newton, something less than a month past, most of his patients had been the victims of gunshot wounds or knifings. The youngster he worked over now had a far greater problem.

Boyd painstakingly bound the boy's ribcage in a tight harness, easing a roll of bandage under his back and around again. The youth's face was ashen, almost chalky, and a bruise the color of rotten plums covered his chin. But that wasn't what concerned the doctor. Even as he worked, he listened, and what he heard was far from encouraging. The boy's breathing was labored, more a hoarse wheezing, and a telltale pinkish froth bubbled at the corners of his mouth. Boyd had seen the symptoms plenty of times after the war, back in Alabama. It was the great ravager. Slow and insidious, without the swift mercy of a rifled slug or a steely knife.

Finished with the bandaging, Gass Boyd once again took out his stethoscope and placed it on the youngster's chest. He listened intently, moving the instrument from spot to spot, wanting desperately to be wrong. But he heard nothing that changed his diagnosis.

Then he grunted sourly to himself. At this stage it ceased being diagnosis. It became, instead, prognosis.

Folding the stethoscope, he placed it in his bag, snapped the catch shut, and stood. Just for a moment he studied the boy, seeing him for the first time as more than a body with sundry ailments and bruises. Hardly more than eighteen. If that. Haggard, hollow-cheeked, gaunt. A face of starved innocence. One of God's miscalculations. Or perhaps the immortal bard had been right after all. Maybe the gods did make wanton sport of men.

Boyd heard rustling behind him and turned to find the Irishman out of his chair on his feet. Their eyes locked and the doctor had a fleeting moment of wonder about this strange man. Beat a boy half to death and then turn a town upside down to save his life. It was a paradox. Classic in its overtones. From a clinical standpoint, perhaps one of the more interesting phenomena in man's erratic tomfoolery.

The doctor set aside such thoughts and came back to the business at hand. "Mr. McCluskie, the boy has a couple of broken ribs and a badly bruised chin. Fortunately your blow didn't catch him in the nose or he might've looked like a bull-dog the rest of his life."

"Then he'll be all right?"

"I didn't say that."

McCluskie's mouth tightened. "What're you gettin' at, Doc?"

"The boy has consumption of the lungs. Rather advanced case, I'd say."

"Consumption?" McCluskie's glance flicked to the bed and back again. "You sure?"

Gass Boyd sighed wearily. "Take my word for it, Mr. McCluskie. The boy has consumption. He's not long for this world."

The Irishman stared at him for what seemed a long while. When he finally spoke his voice had changed somehow. Gentler, perhaps. Not so hard.

"How long?"

Dr. Boyd shrugged. "It's difficult to say. Six months. A year, perhaps. I wouldn't even hazard a guess beyond that."

"Guess? Hell, Doc, I'm not askin' for guesses. He's just a kid. Don't it strike you that somebody punched his ticket a little bit early?"

"Mr. McCluskie, it's an unfortunate fact of life that God plays dirty pool. All too often the good die young. I've never found any satisfactory answer to that, and I doubt that anyone ever will."

"What you're sayin' is that you've given up on him. Written him off."

Far from being offended, the physician found himself fascinated. McCluskie was a strange and complex man, and the irony of the situation was inescapable. Within a matter of minutes he had run the gauntlet of emotions. From hangdog guilt to concern to outraged indignation. Right now he was gripped by a sense of frustrated helplessness, and the only response he knew was to lash out in anger. It was as if this big hulk of a man had unwittingly revealed a part of himself. The part that was raw and vulnerable and rarely saw the light of day.

"I've hardly written him off, Mr. McCluskie. Matter of fact, I'll look in at least twice a day until we have him back on his feet. He's underfed and weak as a kitten, and we have to get his strength built up. Unless things take a drastic turn for the better, I'd judge he won't set foot out of that bed for at least two weeks."

Boyd tactfully avoided any mention of the beating the youngster had taken. There was no need. The punishment absorbed by the frail body was apparent and spoke for itself. McCluskie could scarcely bear to look at the bed, and the loathing he felt for himself showed in his eyes. Watching him, it occurred to the doctor that victims weren't always the ones swathed in bandages. The Irishman's shame at having thrashed a sickly boy would endure far longer than a broken rib or a bruised chin.

McCluskie still hadn't said anything, as if his anger had been blunted by the doctor's unruffled manner. After a moment Boyd gathered his bag and nodded toward the boy. "I've given him a dose of laudanum, so he should rest easy through the night. I'll come by first thing in the morning and see how he's doing."

"Thanks, Doc. I'm—" The Irishman faltered, having difficulty with the words. "Sorry I talked out of turn."

"Completely understandable. No apologies necessary." Boyd smiled, clamped his hat on his head, and crossed the room. But at the door he turned and looked back. "There is one thing, though. If you don't mind my asking. What prompted you to bring the boy here to your room? Instead of over to my office."

McCluskie blinked, taken off guard by a question he hadn't as yet asked himself. "Why, I can't rightly say." He took a swipe at his mustache and shrugged, fumbling with a thought which resisted words. "Just seemed like the thing to do, I guess."

The doctor studied him a moment with a quizzical look. Then he smiled. "Yes. I can see that it would."

Nodding, he opened the door and stepped into the hall.

The Irishman stared at the door for a long while, overcome with a queer sense of unease. The question hung there, still unanswered, and tried to sort it out in his head.

Why had he brought the kid to his room?

Everything else was clear as a bell. The commotion at the depot. Everybody running and shouting and yelling bloody murder at the top of their lungs. Hansberry bleating some asinine nonsense about train robbers, and the little crowd scattering like a bunch of quail. Then later, Spivey and the judge raking him over the coals for coldcocking Tonk Hazeltine. And later still, somebody carting the deputy off like a side of beef. Somewhere in all the fussing and moaning he'd even managed to get the strongbox over to the bank. That part he remembered clearly. But there was just a big blank spot where the kid was concerned. For the life of him, he couldn't recall when or how he'd gotten the kid to his room.

Or why.

Returning to his chair, he sat down and tried to muddle it through. But it was hard sledding, and all uphill. Distantly, as through a cloudy glass, he got an impression of sending Jack off to fetch the doctor. Then something else. Something to do with Spike.

That must have been when he was carrying the kid across Main toward the hotel.

But it still didn't answer the question. The one Doc Boyd had started rattling around in his head. The one that even now didn't make any sense.

Why the hotel? Why *his* room?

McCluskie reached for the whiskey glass and his eyes automatically went to the bed. Jesus! The kid was nothing but a bag of bones. Didn't hardly put a dent in the mattress. Just laid there wheezing and spewing those little bubbles. Like he was—

The rap at the door startled McCluskie clean out of his chair. He crossed the room in two strides and threw open the door. Just for a moment nothing registered. Then those green eyes nailed him and everything came into focus all of a sudden.

It was Belle.

"Well don't just stand there, you big lummox. Let me in."

Wordlessly he stepped aside, his head reeling. He

couldn't have been more surprised if she had materialized out of a puff of smoke.

Belle sailed into the room and whirled on him. "I almost didn't come, you know. Not until Spike told me—"

"Spike?"

"—about the kid."

She stopped and gave him a funny look. "Are you drunk, or what? You did send Spike to get me, didn't you?"

"Yeah, I guess so."

"You guess so?" One eyebrow lifted and she inspected him with closer scrutiny. "Mike, are you all right? You look sort of green around the gills."

Suddenly it all came back to him in a rush. As if somebody had wiped the window clean and he could see it again. The way it had been in those last moments when he walked away from the depot with the kid in his arms.

"Sure I sent Spike. The kid was bad hurt and I didn't know what kind of sawbones they had in this jerkwater burg. You've patched up more men than most of these quacks anyway, so I didn't figure it would hurt nothin' for you to have a looksee."

She gave him that queer look again, still a little leery. "Well, as long as I'm here I might as well inspect the damages." She turned toward the bed. "Where's Doc Boyd? Didn't he show?"

"Yeah, he just left a little while ago."

"What was the verdict? Castor oil and mustard plaster?"

McCluskie had no chance to answer. Belle stopped short of the bed and uttered a sharp gasp. In the pale cider glow of the lamp the boy looked like he had been embalmed. Her eyes riveted on the bandages and the bruised chin and the froth at the corners of his mouth. Her back went stiff as a poker and she mumbled something very unladylike under her breath. Suddenly galvanized, she wheeled around, and green-fire shot out of her eyes in a smoky sizzle.

"You miserable excuse for a man! Is that how you earn your keep? Beating up kids for the Santa Fe?"

"Belle, it's not like it looks. The kid swung on me—"

"Swung on you! My God, Mike, that boy doesn't have enough strength to kill a fly."

"I know that now." He flushed and went on lamely. "But it was dark out there and I couldn't tell. I just knew he was swingin' on me."

"So you let him have the old McCluskie thunderbolt." Her stare was riddled through with scorn. "You must feel real proud of yourself. Why aren't you down at the saloon telling the boys all about your big fight?"

McCluskie's shoulders sagged imperceptibly, and he had trouble meeting her gaze. They stood like that for a moment, frozen in silence. Then, quite without warning, Belle felt her anger start to ebb. Something had just become apparent to her. The big Irishman was ashamed. Really ashamed! This was none of his slick dodges. Those cute little tricks he'd always used to get around her temper. He was genuinely shamed by what he had done. Which rocked her back on her heels.

So far as she knew, Mike McCluskie had never apologized to anybody for anything in his entire life.

Much less hung his head and looked mortified to boot.

Curiously, the question she'd been saving for later no longer needed to be asked. She knew why the kid was here. In this room. Laid out in Mike's bed.

But the knowing left her in something of a quandary. One question had been answered yet others were popping through her head like a string of firecrackers. Questions she had never before even considered about the Irishman.

Suddenly it came to her that perhaps she wasn't as good a judge of men as she had thought. Maybe she'd been running a sporting house too long. Saw things not as they were but distorted and flawed, like a cracked mirror.

She took a closer look at Mike McCluskie.

What she saw was different from what she had seen before. Or perhaps different wasn't the right word. Maybe it was just all there, finally complete. Like a jigsaw puzzle that had at last had the missing parts fitted into place.

She decided to withhold judgment for the moment. "What did Doc have to say about the kid?"

"Couple of busted ribs and a sore jaw."

Belle darted a skeptical glance back toward the bed. "That's all?"

"No, not just exactly." McCluskie swallowed hard. "Doc says he's got lung fever. Consumption."

She just stared at him, unblinking. After a while she managed to talk around the lump in her throat. "He's sure?"

"Sure enough. Said the kid had a year at the outside. Leastways if you're partial to bettin' longshots."

She turned and stepped nearer the bed. Her eyes

went over the frail, emaciated boy, missing nothing. Hair the color of cornsilk, dirty and ragged, but bleached out by the sun. A sensitive face, with wide-set eyes and a straight nose, and the jawbone squared off in a resolute line. Large bony hands with fingers that were curiously slim and tapering. Like those of a piano player. Or a cardsharp. Or a surgeon.

Or any one of a hundred things this kid would never live to become.

Belle jumped, scared out of her wits, as the pale blue eyes popped open. They reminded her of carpenter's chalk, only with a glaze of fresh ice over the top. But the boy didn't see her. His face mottled in dark reddish splotches, and he started sucking for wind in a hoarse, dry rattle. Belle didn't think, she simply reacted.

"He's choking, Mike! Sit him up."

McCluskie reached the bed in one stride, slipping his arms beneath the youngster, and lifted him to a sitting position. Belle wrenched the boy's mouth open, prying his tongue out, and began gently massaging his Adam's apple. Suddenly the boy heaved, his guts pumping, and went into a coughing spasm that shook the entire bed. Globs of sputum and scarlet-tinged mucus shot out of his mouth and nose, and for a moment they thought he was vomiting his life away right in their arms. Then the coughing slacked off, gradually subsiding, and a spark of color came back to his face. The film slowly faded from his eyes and he slumped back, exhausted. The attack had run its course, but he was still laboring for each breath.

Belle plumped up both pillows and wedged them

in behind him. McCluskie eased him back, so that he rested against the pillows in a half-sitting position. Feeling somewhat drained themselves, they just stood there watching him, uncertain what to do next.

Suddenly the boy's lids fluttered and they found themselves staring into the blue eyes again. Only this time they were clear, if not fully alert. The youngster's lips moved in a weak whisper. "Am I back in the hospital?"

McCluskie exchanged puzzled glances with Belle, then shook his head. "You're in a hotel room, kid. We brought you here from the train depot."

The boy closed his eyes and for a minute they thought he was asleep. Then he was looking at them again. Focusing at last on the Irishman. "You the one that clobbered me?"

McCluskie nodded sheepishly. "Thought you was somebody else."

The kid's mouth parted in a sallow grin. "You got a good punch."

McCluskie smiled. The button had plenty of sand, even flat on his back. "What's your name, bucko? Got any family we could get word to?"

"Just me. Nobody else."

"Yeah, but what's your name?"

"Kinch." The boy's eyelids went heavy, drooping, and slowly closed. "Kinch Riley."

The words came in a soft whisper as the laudanum again took hold. Breathing somewhat easier, he drifted off into a deep sleep.

They watched him for a long while, saying nothing. Oddly enough, though they hadn't touched since Belle entered the room, they felt a closeness unlike anything in the past. Almost as if the boy, in some curious way, had bridged a gap in time and space.

At last McCluskie grunted, and his voice was a shade huskier than usual. "Belle, something damned queer happened to me tonight. I've been in brawls, knife fights, shootouts—and afterward I always remembered every minute of it. Every little detail. But tonight—after I slugged the kid—it's all fuzzy. Just comes back to me in bits and snatches. That's one for the books, isn't it?"

She put her arm around his waist and laid her head on his shoulder. "Mister, would you buy a girl a drink?"

The Irishman pulled her close, warmed by her nearness and the scent from her hair. But his eyes were still on the kid.

Then it struck him. The name.

Riley.

Sweet Jesus on the Cross! No wonder he was a gutsy little scrapper.

The kid was Irish.

SIX

McCluskie rode past the stockyards, letting the sorrel mare set her own pace. Now that they were headed back to the livery stable she was full of ginger, apparently cured of her tendency to balk and fight the reins. Several times throughout the day he'd seriously considered the possibility that he had rented a mule disguised as a horse. Along toward midday he started wishing for a pair of the roweled spurs favored by Texans, and would have gladly sunk them to the haft in the mare's flanks. Even coming back from Wichita the hammerhead had acted just like a woman. Wanted her own way and pitched a regular fit when she didn't get it.

The Irishman had ridden out of Newton early that morning on the pretext of inspecting the track crew west of town. While he could have hitched a ride on a switch-engine, he let it drop at the hotel and again at the stables that he felt like a hard day in the saddle. Just to work out the kinks and melt off a bit of the lard from city living. The truth was, he had an absolute loathing for horses. Having served under Sherman during the late war, his rump had stayed galled the better part of three years. Upon being mustered out he had sworn off horses as a mode of transportation for the remainder of his life.

Still, renting a horse was the only practical dodge he could think of for a flying trip to Wichita. It had to be done in one day so as not to arouse the suspicions of Spivey and his cronies. Heading west, he had crossed Sand Creek, passed the stockyard, and kept on a couple of miles farther before turning back southeast. Except for the iron-jawed mare, the twenty miles to Wichita had proved uneventful. There he had quickly hunted down Meade and Grieffenstein, and managed to gain entrance to their offices under an assumed name.

The promoters had been elated when he revealed his identity and the purpose of his call. Although deeply enmeshed in a financial conspiracy with the Santa Fe, they had been kept virtually in the dark by the brass. They knew only that someone would be sent to Newton, and that when the time seemed ripe, they would be contacted.

Some six months past the Santa Fe had entered into an agreement with the partnership of Meade and Grieffenstein. They were to organize a railroad between Wichita and Newton, and float a county bond issue for its construction. Once it was operating, the Santa Fe would buy them out at a tidy profit. The pact was struck and now the vote on the bond issue was less than a month away. The partners had the political muscle to control the southern townships, Wichita in particular, but the upper part of Sedgwick

County still had them worried. Unless the referendum carried, the Wichita & Southwestern railroad would simply evaporate in a puff of dust, and McCluskie's message brought with it a measure of reassurance.

His orders were to establish himself in Newton working undercover as long as practical, and to influence the vote of the northern townships to whatever degree possible. Wherever divisive tactics would work, he was to drive a wedge between the town leaders, splitting them on the bond issue. The sporting crowd, with whom he enjoyed a certain reputation, was to be cultivated on the sly. Hopefully, their ballots could be controlled in a block and provide the swing vote in Newton itself. Further than that, he was instructed to give the promoters any help they might request. But within certain limits. Money and muscle were not included in the bargain.

Retracing his steps across the buff Kansas prairie, McCluskie had hit the tracks a few miles west of the stockyards and turned the mare toward Newton. So far as anyone would know, he had spent the day in the Santa Fe camp, performing some errand for the head office brass. Which was stretching the truth only in terms of time and place. The errand had been real enough, if not precisely as reported.

Now, entering the outskirts of town, he was reminded again of the Wichita promoters. They were a shifty pair, well versed in the rules of the game, and the Irishman had come away with the impression that they still had a few dazzlers left to be played. After years of rubbing elbows with grifters and bunco artists, he had an instinct for such things. Meade and

Grieffenstein were about to sound the death knell on lively little Newton.

Thinking about it as he passed the depot, McCluskie grunted with disgust. All of the skulduggery and underhanded shenanigans left him with a sour taste in his mouth. While he could play the game well enough, it went against the grain. Yet, when it got down to brass tacks, his assignment in Newton was hardly a new role. In a moment of sardonic reflection, it occurred to him that his life had been little more than a lie since the day he headed west.

After the war he had returned to New York, colder and leaner, a man brutalized by the bloodbath that had ended at Appomattox. But he quickly discovered that not all of the casualties had taken place on the battlefield. Only months before, while he rode in the vanguard of Sherman's march to the sea, his wife and small son had been killed in a street riot. Somehow, in those last frenetic days of the war, the army had failed to notify him of their deaths. The homecoming he had dreamed of and longed for during the fighting became instead a ghoulish nightmare. In a single instant, standing dumbstruck before his landlady in Hell's Kitchen, he became both a widower and a bereaved father. Kathleen and Brian, the boy he had never seen, simply ceased to exist.

The blow shook him to the very core of his being. On a hundred killing grounds, from Bull Run to Savannah, he had seen men slaughtered. Grown cold and callous to the sight of death. Accounted for a faceless legion of Johnny Rebs himself. Killing them grimly and efficiently, unmoved toward the end by the bloody handiwork of his saber. Thoroughly ac-

customed to watching men fall before his gun,
screaming and splattered with gore like squealing pigs
in a charnel house. But the death of his wife and son
left him something less than a man. Cold as a stone,
and with scarcely more feeling.

Informed that the riot had occurred at a political
rally, he investigated further and unearthed a chilling
fact. Kathleen and the boy had been innocent bystand-
ers, in the wrong place at the wrong time. Caught up
in a brawl deliberately staged by the ward boss of an
opposing faction. It was simply another Irish donnybrook, political rivals battling for control of the ward,
except that this time it had claimed the lives of three
men. And a woman who happened by with her small
son.

That very night McCluskie sought out the ward
boss and beat him to death with his fists. Afterward,
certain to be charged with murder, he vanished from
Hell's Kitchen and boarded the first train headed west.

The years since had been rewarding after a fashion,
for he was not a man to brood over things dead and
gone. But the ache, though diminished with time, was
still there. For Kathleen, and for the son he had never
seen. It was a part of himself that he kept hidden, and
seldom saw the light of day. Yet as he passed the
depot and reined the mare across the tracks, he was
struck by a curious thought.

He wondered if his boy would have been anything
like Kinch.

Somehow he hoped so, and just exactly why didn't
seem to matter. It was enough that he might have had
a son like the kid. A scrapper who never quit. Never
backed off. A boy to make a man proud.

Dismounting in front of the livery stable, Mc-Cluskie led the mare inside as the sun settled to earth in a fiery splash of gold. Seth Mabry, the proprietor, looked up from shoeing a horse in the dingy smithy set back against the far wall. When he saw that it was the Irishman, he dropped his rasp and hurried forward, wiping his hands on the heavy leather apron covering his chest and belly.

"Well, Mr. McCluskie. You made a day of it. I was just startin' to wonder if you was gonna get back in time for supper."

"Make it a practice never to miss a meal," Mc-Cluskie replied handing over the reins. "Little habit I picked up right after I got weaned."

Mabry's stomach jounced with a fat man's hearty mirth. "Good way to be, Mr. McCluskie. Never was one to pass up a feed myself. Course, there's them that stays partial to milk even when they're full growed. If y'know what I mean."

"Been there myself, Mr. Mabry. Nothin' suits better than going back to the well when your throat gets dry."

"Now ain't that a fact!" The blacksmith squashed a horsefly buzzing about the hairy bristles of his arm. "Say, I didn't even think to ask. Hope Sally gave you that workout you was lookin' for. She's got a lot of sass when she gets to feelin' her oats."

McCluskie snorted and shot the mare a dark look. "Sass don't hardly fit the ticket. She's got a jaw like a cast-iron stove. 'Stead of a quirt you ought to give people a bung starter when you rent her out."

"Just like a woman, ain't it, Mr. McCluskie? Never seen one yet that wasn't bound and determined to make a monkey of a man. Part of bein' female, I guess. Now, you take my wife—"

"Thanks all the same, but I'll pass. Hell, I had enough trouble just handlin' your horse."

The blacksmith was still laughing when McCluskie went through the door and turned down Main Street. Striding along the boardwalk, he almost collided with Randolph Muse in front of the Cattlemen's Exchange. The judge came tearing out of the bank as if his pants were on fire, and McCluskie had to haul up short to keep from bowling him over. It occurred to the Irishman that Muse never seemed to walk. His normal gait was sort of a hitching lope, like a centipede racing back to its hideout.

"Afternoon, Mr. McCluskie." The judge squinted against the sun, grinning, and his store-bought teeth gave off a waxy sheen. "Looks like you had a hard day's ride somewhere."

McCluskie swatted his shirt, raising a small cloud of dust. "Yeah, rode out to have a looksee at the track gang west of town."

"Everything proceeding smoothly, I trust."

"Right on schedule, Judge. Laying 'em down regular as clockwork."

"Good! Good!" They walked on a few paces together and Muse rolled his eyes around in a sidewise glance. "Don't suppose you heard any word about our competition? That Wichita bunch, I mean."

"Can't say as I did, your honor. Most likely they're keepin' their secrets to themselves."

"Well keep your ear to the ground, my boy. Ear to the ground! We need all the information we can get on those rascals."

"I'll do that very thing, Judge. Fellow never knows where he'll turn up an interestin' little tidbit."

"Precisely. Couldn't have said it better myself." Muse took to the street and angled off toward the Lone Star. "I'd ask you to join me in a drink, but I've got a matter of business to discuss with Bob. Say, how is that lad of yours doing? Up and around, is he?"

"Gettin' friskier every day. I figure he'll be ready to try his legs just any time now."

"Excellent. Bring him around to see me. Sounds like a boy with real grit."

Muse turned away with a wave of his hand, kicking up little spurts of dust as he churned along. The Irishman chuckled softly to himself, struck again by the wonder of wee men obsessed with themselves and their wee plans. Passing Horner's Store, he stepped off the boardwalk and headed toward the tracks.

Newt Hansberry waved from the depot platform, but McCluskie merely returned the wave and kept going. This was one time he simply couldn't be bothered with the gossipy station master, or the Santa Fe for that matter. He'd earned his pay for the day and had a sore butt to prove it. The whole lot of them could swing by their thumbs for one night. It was high time he cut the wolf loose and had himself a little fling. Maybe even resurrect that card game with Dandy John and the boys.

The thought came and went with no real conviction. Tonight he'd be doing the same thing he had done every night for the last week. Sitting up with the kid. Just jawboning and swapping yarns till it was bedtime and he could sneak off for a quick one over at the Gold Room.

Not that he begrudged the kid those evenings. Truth was, he sort of enjoyed it. The button had more spunk than a three-legged bulldog, and oddly enough, he'd never felt so proud of anybody in his life. Judge Muse had called it grit, but that didn't hardly fit the ticket. The kid had enough sand in his craw to put them all in the shade. With a little to spare.

Doc Boyd had declared it nothing short of remarkable. The way the kid had perked up and started regaining his strength. Almost as if he had pulled himself up by his own bootstraps. Somehow refused to knuckle under. The sawbones had put a fancy handle on it—the instinct to survive—but McCluskie knew better. It was just plain old Irish moxie, with a streak of stubbornness thrown in on the side. The Gaelic in a man didn't let go without a fight, and Kinch Riley had been standing at the head of the line when they passed out spunk.

Already the color had returned to his face, and he'd lost that skin and bones look. Mostly due to Belle stuffing him full of soup and broth and great pitchers of fresh milk. Every day his spirits improved a notch or two, and he had even started talking about getting out of bed. Doc Boyd had put the quietus on that fast enough, leastways for the time being. But one thing was plain as hell. That kid wouldn't let himself be bound to a bed much longer. Not unless they strapped him down and hid his boots.

Thinking about it, McCluskie had to give most of the credit to Belle. She spent the better part of each day with the kid, returning to her house only when it was time for the evening rush to start. Along with hot food and fresh milk she also dispensed a peck of good cheer. Her sense of humor was sort of on the raw side, but she had a way of joshing the kid that made him light up like a polished apple. Maybe it was just Belle's maternal instinct showing through, but whatever it was, it worked. The kid lapped it up as fast as she could dish it out, and it was her gentle nudging that had finally started him talking.

At first, he had been reluctant to say much about himself. Just his name and the fact that he had no kin. But day by day Belle had wormed her way into his confidence, and when he finally let go it turned out to be a real tearjerker. Even Belle had got that misty look around the eyes, and a couple of times had to interrupt so she could blow her nose.

The kid made it short and sweet, just the bare bones. His folks were from Chicago and had been killed in a fire shortly after he turned seventeen. Afterward, working in the stockyards, he had heard about the Kansas cowtowns and decided to come west. His coughing spells got worse, though, riding the rods. He didn't think much about it at first, because he'd had similar attacks off and on over the past couple of years. But train smoke evidently didn't set well with his lungs and in Kansas City he ended up in a charity ward. The doctors there were a friendly bunch, but they hadn't pulled any punches. They told him what he was up against, and just about what he could expect. Once he was back on his feet, he'd skipped out before anybody got ideas about putting him in a home somewhere. He figured he might as well see the elephant while he had time and he started west again. Things got a little hazy after that, except for being chased and the one haymaker he'd thrown in the Newton rail yard. The next thing he knew, he woke up in Mike's bed.

Later, the Irishman talked it over with Belle and they decided that it was a little more than the luck of the draw. The kid's cards were being dealt from a cold deck, and it was going to be a rough hand to play out alone. McCluskie had surprised himself by volunteering to look after the kid. Just till he got his pins back under him.

Belle wasn't the least bit surprised, though. Not any more. She had laughed and said that it merely confirmed her suspicions. Beneath his stony composure he was all whipped cream and vanilla frosting. In other words, Irish to the core, and a born sucker when it came to siding with an underdog. Then she'd taken him up to her room and come very near to ruining him. When he finally crawled out of her place next morning, he'd felt limp as a dishrag. But good. Restored somehow. Better than he had felt in more than a year.

Now, crossing the hotel lobby, McCluskie had to chuckle to himself as he thought back on it. That was one thing about Belle. Any tricks her girls knew, she knew better, and she could just about cripple a man when her spring came unwound.

Whistling tunelessly, he walked down the short hallway and entered his room. Or what had once been his room. It was the kid's now. He merely kept his clothes there and paid the rent. For the past week he'd been staying at Belle's, and getting himself worn to a frazzle in the process.

The kid was propped up in bed riffling a deck of cards on his lap. When McCluskie came through the door, he looked around and broke out in a wide smile.

"Mike! We was just about to send the cavalry out lookin' for you."

"Evenin', sport." The Irishman sailed his hat in the general direction of a coat rack and walked to the washstand. "Who's we?"

"Why, Belle and me. She just left a minute ago." Kinch laughed and shook his head. "She's a pistol, ain't she? Said she couldn't wait no longer or them cowhands'd be bustin' down the doors."

McCluskie glanced up at him in the mirror. "Belle said that?"

"Yeah, sure. Why?"

"Nothin'." He peeled his shirt and tossed it on a chair. "Guess she figures you're a shade older'n you look."

The boy reared back and scowled indignantly. "Well hell, Mike, I'm pushin' eighteen, y'know. Betcha when you was my age you'd been around plenty."

"Kid, when I was your age I was a hundred years old." McCluskie poured water in a washbowl and began his nightly birdbath. "But that don't cut no ice one way or the other. Now, c'mon, own up to it. You've never had a woman in your life, have you?"

Kinch went red as beet juice and fumbled around for a snappy comeback. "Well I come close a couple of times, don't you worry yourself about that. I'm not as green as I look."

"Hey, cool down. I wasn't rubbin' your nose in it. Just meant there's a few gaps in your education, that's all. Soon's you get the lead back in your pencil we'll have to arrange some lessons down at Belle's."

It took a moment for the meaning to register, and then the youngster burst out in a whooping belly laugh. Suddenly his face drained of color and the laugh turned to a racking cough. The attack was fairly short, and his sputum was no longer flecked with blood, but the pain was clearly evident in his face. Still, he tended to accept it with a stoicism beyond his years. Though hardly an old friend, pain was a familiar companion these days, and lying around on his backsides had given him plenty of time to think it out. There wasn't much to be gained in feeling sorry for himself—and moaning about it wouldn't change anything—so he might as well make the best of what time he had. Besides, what with one thing and another, he'd come out smelling like a rose anyway. It wasn't just everybody that got themselves hooked up with a slick article like the Irishman. Not by a damn-sight, it wasn't.

As his cough slacked off, the boy glanced up and saw McCluskie watching him intently. He forced a smile and went back to shuffling the cards. "Y'know, Belle says that with my hands I wouldn't have no trouble at all learnin' how to make these pasteboards sit up and talk."

McCluskie finished splashing and started toweling himself dry. "Seems like Belle's just chock full of ideas for you."

"She's some talker, awright. Smart, too." Kinch cut the deck and began dealing dummy hands of stud on the bed. "But she's right about one thing. I ain't gonna be tied to this bed forever, and I gotta get myself lined up with some kind of work. It's real white of you, footin' all the bills like this, but I'm used to payin' my own freight."

McCluskie stifled the temptation to smile. Sometimes the kid was so damned serious it was all he could do to keep a straight face. Sat there chewing his lip and frowning, like a little old man puzzling over some problem that had confounded the world's scholars. For a button, he was a prize package. In spades.

"Well now, I'll tell you, sport—I've been giving that some thought myself. The Santa Fe has got me wore down to a stump pullin' their chestnuts out of the fire. Just never seems to be no end to it. Truth is, I've been thinkin' of hirin' myself an assistant, and I got an idea you might just fit the ticket. Course, the wages wouldn't be much to start, but it'd get you by."

"Cripes, I ain't worried about that, Mike. Long as I got three squares and a bed, I figure I'm livin' high on the hog."

"You mull it over some. No hurry. When you get back on your feet if you still like the idea, we'll give it a whirl."

McCluskie pulled a fresh shirt out of the bureau and started putting it on. The boy was watching his every move with renewed interest, and a quizzical look came over his face all of a sudden.

"Say, Mike, I ain't never got around to it, but there's something I been meanin' to ask you. How'd you get that scar on your belly?"

The Irishman glanced down at the jagged weal running from his ribs to his beltline, then went on buttoning the shirt. "Some hardcase came at me with a knife one night in Abilene."

"God A'mighty! What happened to him?"

"Nothin' special. Just a regular ten-dollar funeral."

Kinch's eyes went round as saucers and he sat there staring, the deck of cards forgotten.

With his shirt tucked in, McCluskie deliberated a moment and then gave the boy a questioning look. "Listen, bud, if you and me start workin' together, I want you to quit using that word *ain't* so much. It's not the word that bothers me, you understand, but it reminds me of somebody that rubs my fur the wrong way. Likely you'll meet him first time we're over at the depot."

The youngster ducked his head. "Sure, Mike. Anything you say. Won't be no trouble at all."

McCluskie grinned. "Tell you what. I'll go get us a supper tray, and after we eat, maybe I'll show you how to make them cards sit up and say *bow wow.*"

Kinch's face lit up and he got busy shuffling the cards. But as the Irishman went through the door he sobered with a sudden thought and gave a loud yell.

"Tell 'em to hold the milk! Belle's got me swimmin' in the stuff."

SEVEN

The day was bright as brass, a regular Kansas scorcher. Lazy clouds hung suspended against the blue muslin of the sky, and the sun hammered down with the fury of an open forge. The air was still, without a hint of breeze, and across the prairie shimmering heat waves drifted soft as woodsmoke. Already the morning was a small slice of hell, and by noon the blazing fireball overhead would wilt anything that moved.

But it was the kind of day McCluskie liked. Clear and windless, and hot enough to keep a man's joints oiled with sweat. Perfect for burning powder, and testing himself against his keenest rival.

The one that dwelled within himself.

The Irishman came each morning to the rolling plains north of town. There, in a dry wash fissured through the earth's bowels, he played a game. The object was to beat his shadow on the gully wall. To draw and fire the Colt Navy a split second faster than his darkened image. Yet that was only part of the game. For while his shadow was allowed to miss, he granted himself no such edge.

Each slug must strike the target—a kill shot—or the game was lost.

McCluskie had been playing this game for three years, since the spring of '68 when he came west with the K&P. Not unlike most things he did, it was calculated and performed with solemn deliberation. Broiling his guts out with a track gang, laying rails across the parched Kansas plains, he had decided to make something better of himself than a common laborer. Watching and waiting, he studied the matter for a time, and concluded that the job of railway guard would be the first step. That required a certain aptitude with a gun, and with no one to school him, he taught himself. He invented the game and began practicing in his off time. Through trial and error he perfected the rudiments of what would later become rigid discipline, and shortly thereafter, his newly acquired skill came to the attention of company officials.

Later, after he had killed three men, people stopped joshing him about the game. They had seen the results, and the greatest skeptic among them became a devout believer.

McCluskie, along with Hickok and Hardin and a handful more, was a man to be cultivated. Befriended or won over somehow. Failing that, it was best to simply stay clear of him.

Even now, the Irishman still practiced the game religiously. Since killing the Quinton brothers, when they attempted to rob a K&P express car the summer of '69, there had been no occasion to draw the Colt in anger. His name was known, and anyone deadly enough to match his skill had better sense than to try. But this in no way diverted him from the game. The world was full of men too dumb, or too hotheaded, to back down, and in his trade, the risk of coming up against these hardcases was always there. With spartan discipline, he practiced faithfully, seven days a week. It was a demanding craft, one that allowed no margin for error. A man's first mistake might well be his last, and the prize for second place wasn't a gold watch.

McCluskie had never begrudged the time demanded by the game. Curiously, he'd always thought of it as an investment. Money in the bank. Better to have it and not need it than to need it and not have it. Which in his line of work made a pretty fair maxim all the way round.

So he practiced and improved and waited.

The past week had been a little different, though. Generally he played the game solitaire, but lately he'd started bringing Kinch along. The boy was recuperated, at least as much as he ever would be, and Doc Boyd had agreed that fresh air and sunshine were curatives in their own right. McCluskie enjoyed the company, and the kid seemed fascinated by the game, so the mornings had become a special time for them both.

There was only one thing that bothered the Irishman. Puzzled him in a way he couldn't quite fathom. The kid had been watching him for days now and never once had he asked to fire the pistol. Hadn't even asked to touch it, or evidenced the slightest curiosity in how it worked. Apparently his only interest was in the game itself, trying to judge who was the fastest. Man or shadow.

All of which seemed a bit queer to McCluskie. Most boys would have given their eyeteeth to sit in on these sessions. More to the point, though, they would have broken out in a case of the blue swivets waiting to get their hands on the gun. To see how good they could do. To learn. To feel the Colt buck and jump and spit lead. That's what he would have expected from any kid old enough to wear long pants.

But Kinch just hung back, watchful as a hawk, plainly satisfied to remain nothing more than a spectator.

McCluskie couldn't figure it, but as yet he hadn't pushed it either. There were lots of reasons that could make the kid shy off. None of them worthwhile from a man's standpoint, and some of them too repulsive even to consider. But he left it alone, saying nothing. The kid would come around in his own time, and if he didn't, there would be plenty of chances to find out why.

This was the fifth morning Kinch had tagged along, and by now the boy was accustomed to the ritual. Squatting down against one side of the gully, he observed silently as McCluskie set about the game. The first step was a target, and for this they had brought along a gunnysack stuffed with empty tin cans. The tins were of assorted sizes, mostly pints and quarts. McCluskie had wedged a plank between the walls of the gully about chest high, and on this he arranged five tins at spaced intervals. Then he stepped off ten paces and turned, facing the target. From his pocket he withdrew a double eagle and placed it in his left hand. Ready now, he stood loose and easy, arms hanging naturally at his sides. The only tenseness was in his eyes, and to the watching boy, it seemed that every fiber of his being was concentrated on the five cans.

Like most Westerners, McCluskie carried the Colt high on his hip, with the butt of the gun resting just below waistline. There were those who used tied-down triggers, low-slung holsters, even swivel affairs that allowed a man to twist the gun upward and fire while it was still in the holster. But experience, and three years of watching self-styled badmen commit suicide, had convinced him that such devices were strictly the work of amateurs. Flash-in-the-pan braggarts who thought an edge in speed could overcome a shortness in guts. The place for a gun was where it rode comfortable, easy to reach sitting or standing, and where it came natural to the hand when a man made his move.

The Irishman's left hand opened and the double eagle tumbled out. There was a space of only a split second before it hit the rocky floor of the wash. The metallic ring was the signal, and with it McCluskie's right arm moved. To the naked eye it was merely a blurred motion, but the Colt suddenly appeared in his hand and exploded flame.

The center can leaped off the plank and spun away.

Alternating his shots left to right, McCluskie sent the remaining tins bouncing down the gully. From first shot to last, the whole thing had consumed no more than a half-dozen heartbeats. Working with deliberate speed, McCluskie pulled out powder and ball, and began reloading.

Kinch was no less fascinated than the first time he had seen it happen. There was something magic about it, like a man pulling a rabbit out of a hat. One minute McCluskie was just standing there, and in the blink of an eye the gun was in his hand and whanging tin cans all over the place. It was hard to believe, except that he'd seen it repeated five mornings in a row.

Grinning, he picked up a rock and chunked it at one of the tins. "Better watch it, Mike. The shadow almost caught you that time."

McCluskie grunted, smiling. "Un-huh. Toad's got six toes, too. You keep a sharp lookout, though, sport. Can't let the bogeyman get too close or I'll have to take up cards for a livin'."

The Irishman directed his attention to the cans once more, and for the next half-hour blasted his way through what had become by now a ritualized drill. First, he increased the distance to twenty paces and began walking toward a fresh row of cans. Suddenly he halted in midstride, dropped into a crouch and started firing. Five tins again winged skyward.

Next, he stood with his back to the plank and held his arms in unusually awkward positions. Overhead, out to the side, scratching his nose. The way it might happen if he were taken by surprise. On signal from the coin, he would wheel around and open fire. Again and again he practiced these movements, spinning to the right on one exchange and to the left on another, each time changing the order in which he potted the cans.

Finally, he walked off down the gully a good fifty yards and halted. Turning sideways, he assumed the classic duelist's stance. Thumbing off each shot with precise care, using the sights for the first time, he started on the left and ticked off the cans in sequence. He missed on the last shot.

Kinch felt like the inside of his skull was being donged by the clapper in a church bell. The morning's barrage had left him all but deaf, and reverberations from the staccato bark of the pistol still rang in his ears. But the noise had little to do with the reason for shaking his head. By exact count, the Irishman had fired fifty shots.

He had missed only once. The last can.

While the boy was visibly impressed, McCluskie himself was muttering curses as he walked forward. Granted, it was the best score he'd racked up this week. But it wasn't good enough. Not in this game. The missed shot might have been the very one to put him in a box with a bunch of daisies in his hand. Concentration! That's where he had slipped up. Plain and simple.

Lack of concentration.

The Irishman squatted down beside the boy and began disassembling his pistol. This was something else that fascinated the youngster, the almost reverent care McCluskie lavished on the weapon. Kinch knew that later he would scrub out the black powder residue with soap and hot water. But for now he made do with swabbing a lightly oiled cloth through the barrel and the cylinder chambers.

McCluskie glanced up and smiled at the kid's solemn expression. "Well, bud, we didn't win the war but we scared the hell out of 'em. Still can't figure how I missed that last shot."

"It's important to you, ain't"—he grinned and made a face—"I mean, isn't it?"

McCluskie acted as though he hadn't noted the slip. "Damn right it's important. Not just because it's part of my job, either. Y'know, you're not back in Chicago any more. Out here a man has got to look out for himself."

"Yeah, but they got law in Newton. I mean, it's not like you was off in the mountains somewheres with a bunch of wild animals."

McCluskie snorted and peered down the barrel of the Colt. "Lemme tell you something, sport. The tough things in this life are sort of like takin' a leak. You've got to stand on your own two feet and nobody else can do it for you. That goes double in a place where everybody and his dog carries a gun. The law might arrest your murderer—maybe even hang him—but that's not likely to do you a whole lot of good. Dead's dead, and that's all she wrote."

Kinch picked up a pebble, studying it a moment, then shot it across the gully like a marble. "Belle says you've killed three men."

"Judas Priest, there's nothin' that woman won't talk about, is there?"

The boy gave him a sideways glance, then looked away again. Something was eating at him and it was a while before he could find the right words. "Is it hard to kill a man, Mike?"

"Well, I don't know." The Irishman paused and pulled reflectively at his ear. "Most times you don't think about it when it's happenin'. It's like fightin' off bees. You just do what needs doing to keep from gettin' stung."

"Yeah, but afterward don't you think about it? Maybe wish you hadn't done it?"

"Like feelin' sorry, you mean?"

Kinch nodded, watching him intently.

"What you're talkin' about is all that stuff in the Good Book. Thou shalt not this and that. The way I look at it, guilt is for them that needs it."

"I don't get you."

"Well, it's like this. Some folks are just miserable inside unless they've got something to feel guilty about. Sort of like it'd been bred into 'em, the same as horns on a cow. They're not really happy unless they're sad. All choked up with guilt. Y'see what I mean?"

The boy mulled it over a minute, frowning thoughtfully. "You're sayin' that if they kill a man to keep from gettin' killed, they still feel guilty. Like it was wrong doing it even to save themselves."

"That's about the size of it, I guess."

"But shouldn't you feel sorry, even a little bit? Somehow it don't seem the same as slaughterin' a pig or knockin' a steer in the head."

"Sport, it's not ghosts that haunt our lives. It's people. The live ones are who you've got to worry about. Don't waste your time on the dead. Where they are, it won't make a particle of difference."

Kinch again looked away, troubled by something he couldn't quite come to grips with. The game McCluskie played was fun to watch, the same way there was something grimly fascinating about watching a snake rear back and shake its rattles. But all week something had bothered him about the gun. Not anything he could exactly put his finger on, just a worrisome thought that wouldn't go away. Now he knew what it was.

The game had only one purpose. And it wasn't to perforate tin cans.

Since his little siege in the charity ward back in Kansas City, Kinch had had plenty of time to think. Mostly about death, and especially his own. In some queer sort of way it was as if he and Death had become close acquaintances, without a secret between them. Yet in the closeness came a curious turnabout. It wasn't that death frightened him so much as that life had suddenly become very precious. Each day was somehow special, a thing to be treasured, and every breath his lungs took seemed sweeter than the one before. Death in itself was sort of shrouded, a misty bunch of nothing that even the preachers couldn't explain too well. But the loss of life was very real, something he could understand all on his own. When the candle was snuffed out, everything he was or might have been just stopped. Double ought zero.

The thought of killing someone wasn't just repugnant. It was scary in a way that resisted words. Like killing another man would somehow kill a part of himself. Almost as if the time he had left would be whittled down in the act of stealing from another what he himself prized the most.

Then again, maybe it was like the Irishman said. Life couldn't be all that precious if a man wouldn't fight to save it. Only something of little value was tossed aside lightly, and that didn't include the privilege to go on breathing.

Kinch glanced at the big man out of the corner of his eye. Since the loss of his family a year past he had been drifting aimlessly, with no real goal in mind except to taste life before his time ran out. McCluskie was the first person to show any interest in him, to take the time and trouble to talk with him. Strangely enough, these talks somehow put him in mind of quiet evenings back in Chicago. When he and his father would sit on the tenement stoop and discuss all manner of things. But that was before the fire. And the screaming and smoke and charred stench of death.

He shuddered inside, remembering again how it had been. Then he took hold of himself and wiped the thought from his mind. There was nothing to be gained in living in the past. Just bitter memories and grief and a void that ached to be filled. Here and now, with the Irishman, he had the start of something new. A friendship certainly, otherwise McCluskie would never have taken him in and cared for him and given him a job. But over and above that there was something more. A closeness shared, unlike anything he'd ever known for another man. Except maybe for his father, and even that was somehow different.

Despite McCluskie's brusque manner and gamy joshing he felt drawn to the man. Not that McCluskie treated him as full grown. Nor was it just exactly a father to son kind of thing. Instead, it was something in between, a partnership of sorts, and perhaps that was what made it different. One of a kind. A rare thing, and exciting.

Puzzling over it, Kinch decided on the spur of the moment that he could have picked worse spots than Newton to pile off the train. Lots worse. Truth to tell, getting clobbered by the Irishman might well have been an unusual stroke of luck. They made a pretty good team, and it came to him all of a sudden that he had found something he didn't want to lose. Something damned special. And he wasn't about to rock the boat.

Whichever way the Irishman led, he meant to follow.

McCluskie finished assembling the Colt and started loading it. Seating a ball, he rammed it down and looked over at the kid. "Y'know, there's nothin' stoppin' you from tryin' your hand with this thing. Wouldn't be no trouble at all to show you how it's done. Matter of fact, what with you being my assistant, it might be a good idea. Never yet hurt a man to know one end of a gun from the other."

Kinch uncoiled slowly and got to his feet. "I'll give 'er a try. So long as we stick to shootin' at cans."

"Meanin' you're not ready to try your luck with something that shoots back."

The boy grinned. "I'd just as soon not."

"Bud, I hope it never comes to that. What I said a while ago about guilt and all—I meant that. But it's not much fun killin' a man. Just between us, I could do without it myself."

McCluskie devoted the next hour to demonstrating the rudiments of what he had learned through nearly three years of trial and error. Instructing someone in the use of a gun seemed awkward at first, but he found Kinch an eager pupil. Things he had never before put into words made even more sense when he heard himself explaining it, and the boy's sudden interest gratified him in a way he would never have suspected. Nor did he fully understand it. He was just damned pleased.

Concentration and balance and deliberation. According to the Irishman, these were the sum and substance of firing a pistol accurately. Distractions of whatever variety—movement, sound, even gunfire—must be blocked out of a man's mind. Every nerve in his body must be focused with an iron grip on the target. Almost as if he were blinded to anything except the spot he wanted to hit. Without this intensity of concentration, he would more likely than not throw the shot off. Since the first shot was the one that counted, to waste it was a hazardous proposition at best.

Balance had to do with a man's stance and his aiming of the gun. McCluskie demonstrated by dropping into a crouch, feet slightly apart, and leveling the gun to a point that his arm was about equidistant between waist and shoulder. Each man soon determined the position most natural to himself, but the crouch was essential. It not only made him a smaller target, but more importantly, it centered the gun on his opponent's vitals. The chest and belly. At that point a man forgot the sights and aimed by instinct. Much the same as pointing his finger. With his body squarely directed into the target, and the gun jabbed out as an extension of his finger, he had only to bring his arm level and the slug would strike pretty much dead center every time.

McCluskie paused, mulling over the next part, and tried to frame his words to capture the precise meaning of a single thought.

"Forget about speed. That'll get a man planted quicker'n anything. It's not how fast you shoot or how many shots you get off. What counts is that you hit what you're shootin' at. With the first shot. If you can't learn to do that, then you've got no business carryin' a gun."

Kinch gave him a skeptical look. "You sound like one of them preachers that says 'do as I say, not as I do.' Cripes, I've been sittin' here for a whole week watchin' you whip that thing out like it had grease on it."

"That's because you've been watchin'," McCluskie growled, "instead of payin' attention. You've got fast mixed up with sudden. There's difference, and not understandin' that is what gets a man a one way ticket to the Pearly Gates."

The Irishman leveled his pistol at arm's length. "Right there's where you hesitate before you pull the trigger. But it's only a little hesitation, a fragment of a second. Nothin' a man could count even when he's doing it. Just a split-hair delay to catch the barrel out of the corner of your eye and make sure it's lined up on the target. Then you pull the trigger."

The Colt roared and a can spun off the plank.

"Learn that before you learn anything else. It's the difference between the quick and the dead. Deliberation. Sudden instead of fast. Whatever you want to call it. Just slow down enough so that your first shot counts. Otherwise you might not get a second."

McCluskie positioned the boy only five paces from the plank to start. They worked for a while on stance and gaining a feel for pointing the gun. Then he had the kid hold the Colt down at his side and concentrate on a single can. The label on it showed a bright golden peach.

"Whenever you're ready."

Kinch whipped the gun up and blasted off four shots in a chain-lightning barrage.

The can hadn't moved.

"No goddamnit, you're not listenin'. I said hesitate. Take your time. Hell, any dimdot can stand there and just pull the trigger. Now load up and try it again. Only slow down, for Chrissakes."

The next half-hour was excruciating for both teacher and pupil. The boy fired and loaded four cylinders—twenty shots—before he hit the juicy-looking peach. All the while McCluskie was storming and yelling advice and growing more exasperated with each pull of the trigger. Oddly enough, he seemed madder than if he himself had run out the string of misses.

But something had clicked on that last shot, the hit. Understanding came so sudden that Kinch felt as if his ears had come unplugged. The delay had been there. Right under his fingertips, like a sliver of smoke. He had felt it, sensed that it was waiting on him. Known even before he feathered the trigger that the can would jump.

He reloaded, blocking out McCluskie and the heat and the ringing in his ears. Then he crouched, leveling his arm, and the gun began to buck. Spaced shots, neither slow nor fast, with a mere trickle of time between each report.

Three cans out of five leaped from the plank.

The Irishman just stood there a moment, staring at the punctured tins. Then his mouth creased in a slow smile.

"Well I'll be a sonovabitch. You rung the gong."

EIGHT

—⊐⊓⊓⎧ ⎫⊓⊓⊏—

McCluskie had given the matter of Kinch's birthday considerable thought. The kid was turning eighteen, which was sort of a milestone in a youngster's life. The day he ceased being a boy and set about the business of becoming a man.

Not that a youngster couldn't have fought Indians or rustled cattle or killed himself a couple of men by that time. There were many who had, and lots more who fell shy by only the slimmest of margins. Wes Hardin, who had treed Abilene just last month, was scarcely eighteen himself. Yet, according to newspaper claims, he had even run a sandy on Wild Bill Hickok.

Life west of Kansas City forced a boy to grow up in a hurry. All too often, though, it killed him off before he ever really got started.

Personally, the Irishman had never set much store with this thing of birthdays. The idea of a boy becoming a man just because he'd chalked up a certain number of years seemed a little absurd. That pretty much assumed a kid couldn't cut the mustard, and McCluskie knew different. He had joined the Union army at the advanced age of nineteen, and nobody had ever been called upon to hold his hand. From the opening gun he had pulled his own weight, and when the Rebs finally called it quits, he'd felt like the old man of his outfit.

The killing ground did that. Seared the childish notions out of a boy's head and made him look at things in a different light. Like a man.

McCluskie had learned that lesson the hard way. First hand. When he came west after the war, he was a man stripped of illusions. Life fought dirty in the clinches, so he had discovered, and it didn't pay to give the other fellow an even break. Just as he felt no remorse over the men he had killed in the war, so it was that he felt nothing for the ward boss in Hell's Kitchen, or the three hardcases he had planted in Abilene. There were some people just bound and determined to get themselves killed. The fact that he was the instrument of their abrupt and somewhat unceremonious demise was their lookout, not his. Not by a damnsight. Yet, in some queer way that he'd never really fathomed, he took neither pleasure nor pride in killing. It was like he had told the kid.

It's not much fun killin' a man.

Still, it was one thing to feel a twinge of regret and something else entirely to turn the other cheek. A man tended to his own business and tried not to step on the other fellow's toes. But he also fought his own fights, and anyone who came looking for trouble deserved whatever he got. Whether it was a busted nose or a rough pine box. That's the way the game was played, and while he hadn't made the rules, he wasn't about to break them either. Only dimdots and faint-hearts came west expecting to get a fair shake from the next man, and more often than not, they were the ones who ended up on an undertaker's slab.

Understandably then, McCluskie didn't believe in mollycoddling. The sooner kids learned to wipe their own noses, the better off for all concerned. Curiously enough, though, he had been at some pains to make an event of Kinch's birthday.

The excuses he gave himself were pretty lame. Generally he didn't allow feeling to stand in the way of common sense. He saw himself as a realist in a hard and uncompromising world. A man who met life on its own terms and handed out more licks than he took. Underneath his flinty composure, it grated the wrong way to admit there was still a soft spot he hadn't whipped into line. But he'd never been a man to fool himself, either. It all boiled down to one in-escapable fact.

There wouldn't be any more birthdays for the kid. Eighteen was where the string ran out.

Oddly enough, the Irishman was having a hard time dealing with that. It confused him, this feeling he had for the kid. Part of it had to do with a small boy killed in a street brawl, the one he'd never seen. And he understood that. Accepted it as natural that a man would dredge up old feelings, musty and long buried, and allow a skinny, underfed kid to touch his soft spot. Even a man who made his living with a gun wasn't without a spark of emotion. No matter how many times he'd killed. Or told himself there was nothing on earth that could get under his skin and make him breathe life into thoughts dead and gone. That part held no riddle for him, and he had come to grips with it in his own way.

What bothered him, and left him more than a little bemused, was the extent of his feeling. Somehow the kid had penetrated his soft spot far deeper than he'd suspected at the outset. Little by little, over the course of their weeks together, the youngster had burrowed clean into the core. Like a worm that slowly bores a passage in hard-packed earth. Now the Irishman found himself face to face with something he couldn't quite handle. It was Hell's Kitchen all over again. Only this time he was there. Forced to stand helplessly by, as if his hands were tied, and watch it happen. Almost as though life had felt cheated the first time, and out of spite had summoned him back to observe, at last, the death of a boy.

In some diabolic fashion, the death of his own son.

That evening, when he got to the hotel, Kinch had himself all decked out in a new set of duds. The Irishman had forewarned him that this was the night. After nearly three weeks of taking it easy and soaking up sunshine, it was high time he got his feet wet.

Tonight they were out to see the elephant.

Kinch had splurged like a cowhand fresh off the trail. The wages McCluskie paid weren't princely by any yardstick, but the best at the Blue Front Clothing Store had been none too good. Candy-striped shirt, slouch hat, boots freshly blacked, and a peacock blue kerchief knotted around his neck. He was clean scrubbed and reeked of rose water, and his hair looked like it had been plastered down with a trowel.

McCluskie whistled and gave him the full once

over. "Well now, just looky here. Got yourself all tricked out like it was Sunday-go-to-meetin'."

The boy preened and darted a quick look at himself in the mirror. "Just followin' orders. You said bright-eyed and bushy-tailed."

Damned if I didn't. Sort of took me at my word, too, didn't you?"

"Guess I did, at that. Put a dent about the size of a freight engine in my pocketbook."

The Irishman suddenly remembered the package he'd brought along and thrust it out. "Here. What with it being your birthday and all, I figured you was due a bonus."

"Aw, hell, Mike. You didn't have to buy me nothin'."

The sparkle in the kid's eyes belied his words, and it was all he could do to keep from ripping the package open. Setting it on the dresser, he forced himself to slowly untie the cord and peel back the wrapping paper. Then he removed the box top and his jaw popped open in astonishment.

"Hoooly Moses!"

Inside was a Colt Navy with a gunbelt and holster.

Kinch just stood there, mesmerized by the walnut grips and blued steel and the smell of new leather. After a while McCluskie chuckled and gave him a nudge. "Go ahead, try it on. It's not new, you understand, but she shoots as good as mine. I tried'er out this afternoon."

The boy pulled the rig out of the box as if it were dipped in gold and buckled it around his hips. It fitted perfectly, and he knew without asking that McCluskie had had it special made. There wasn't a store-bought gunbelt the near side of Kingdom Come that wouldn't have swallowed his skinny rump.

The Irishman took his shoulders and positioned him in front of the mirror. "Take a gander at yourself, bud. Don't hardly look like the same fellow, does it?"

Kinch just stared at the reflection in the mirror, dumfounded somehow by the stranger who stared back.

McCluskie grinned. "Much more and you'll bore a hole clean through that lookin' glass. C'mon, say something."

The kid's arm moved and they were both staring down the large black hole of the Colt's snout. The youthful face in the mirror laughed, eyes shining brightly. "D'ya see it?"

"See it?" McCluskie's grin broadened. "That's a damnfool question. What was it I taught you, anyway?"

That the hand's faster than the eye."

"Well you've got your proof right there in that mirror. The fellow you're lookin' at didn't even see it. He's still blinkin'."

While it was a slight exaggeration, McCluskie's comment wasn't far wide of the mark. The truth was, he hadn't seen the kid draw. Nor did it surprise him. Not after the last couple of days in the gully north of town.

The swiftness with which the kid learned was nothing short of incredible. In two weeks he had mastered what some men never absorbed in a lifetime. Part of it was the will to learn, and some of it was McCluskie's dogged insistence on practice. But most of it was simply the boy's hands. Slim and tapered, hardened from work, but with a strength and quickness that was all but unimaginable. What those hands knew couldn't be taught. It was there all along, waiting merely to be trained. Reaction and speed was a gift. Something a man was born with. The rest was purely a matter of practice.

Kinch wasn't as good as he would be. Or as yet anywhere close to McCluskie. But he was fast. Even too fast, perhaps. The best score he'd racked up so far was three out of five cans. While he was fairly consistent, and improving every day, he still hadn't overcome a tendency to rush. Quite plainly, despite the Irishman's constant scolding, he had been bitten by the speed bug.

Still, this obsession with speed wasn't what troubled McCluskie the most. That would pass soon enough. As the kid got better, and gained confidence in himself, he would see that sudden beat fast everytime. The worrisome thing was Kinch's attitude. He still looked on the whole deal as one big game. Just a lark. A sporting event of some sort where the only casualties were a bunch of tin cans.

McCluskie wasn't completely unaware of what lay behind the kid's lighthearted manner. Perhaps any man, faced with the prospect of his own death, would have reacted the same way. Yet it was hard to accept, for it overlooked a salient detail. Places like Newton often pitted a man against something besides tin cans. Something that could shoot back.

Thinking about it now, as Kinch preened in front of the mirror, he wondered if he had done the right thing. Maybe giving the kid a gun wouldn't change anything. That remained to be seen. But one thing was for damn sure. It had put a spark in his eye that wasn't there before, and for the moment, that in itself was enough.

When they left the hotel dusk had already fallen, and the southside was a regular beehive of activity. Trailhands thronged the boardwalk, drifting from dive to dive with the rowdy exuberance of schoolboys playing hooky. Along the street rinky-dink pianos tinkled in witless harmony, and over the laughing and shouting and drunken Rebel yells, it all came together in a calliope of strident gibberish. Every night was Saturday night in Newton, and so long as the Texans' money held out, they flung themselves headlong into a frenetic swirl of cheap whiskey and fast women.

McCluskie angled across the street toward the Gold Room. That seemed like as good a place to start as any, but by no means would it be their last stop. Before introducing the kid to Belle's girls he figured to hit at least three or four dives. Somehow he just couldn't picture the youngster waltzing into a whorehouse stone-cold sober. Better to float his kidneys first, and then let the ladies instruct him in the ancient and noble sport of dip the wick.

They came through the door with Kinch hard on his heels and headed for the bar. Every couple of steps the youngster took a hitch at his gunbelt, as if checking to make sure it was still there. The pistol felt strange and somehow reassuring on his hip, and the temptation to touch it was too much to resist. Had it been a wart between his eyes he wouldn't have been any less conscious of its existence.

Pony Reid greeted them at the bar. "Evenin', Mike.

Kinch. You boys are gettin' an early start, aren't you?"

"Pony, we're out to see the elephant." McCluskie clapped the kid across the shoulders. "Not that you'd remember back that far, but Kinch just turned the corner on eighteen. He's ready to cut the wolf loose and let him howl."

By now everyone in town knew the story on the Irishman's young assistant. They had become all but inseparable, and it required only a moment's observation to see that the kid idolized McCluskie. In the manner of rough-natured men, the sporting crowd had adopted Kinch as one of their own.

"Hell's bells, that calls for a drink!" Reid signaled the barkeep. "Set 'em up for my friends here. Celebration like this has to get started off proper."

The bartender poured out three shots and Reid hoisted his glass. "Kinch, here's mud in your eye. Happy days."

The gambler and McCluskie downed their whiskey neat. Kinch hesitated only a moment and followed suit. When the liquor hit bottom it bounced dangerously, exploding in a series of molten eruptions. His eyes watered furiously and he felt sure smoke would belch out of his ears at any moment. But somehow he managed to hold it down, and after a couple of quick breaths, he gave the older men a weak smile.

"Mighty good drinkin' whiskey. Next one's on me."

"The hell you say!" The Irishman slapped a double eagle on the bar and winked sideways at Pony Reid. "Treat's on me. The rest of the night. Barkeep! Set 'em up again."

Kinch had the sinking sensation that another round might just paralyze him, but he merely grinned and bellied up closer to the bar. This was the first time the Irishman had allowed him anything stronger than a warm beer, and he wasn't about to back off now.

Then, as he lifted the glass again, his nose twitched. Cripes! No wonder they called it coffin varnish. That's what it smelled like. Only worse.

They came through the door of Belle's house arm in arm. Kinch was listing slightly, but still navigating under his own power. This, along with his clear eye and steady speech, had the Irishman a little puzzled. After a whirlwind tour of three saloons in the past two hours he'd fully expected to have the youngster ossified and walking on air. But it hadn't worked out that way.

Apparently the kid had a greater tolerance for whiskey than he'd suspected. That or a hollow leg.

Halting in the entranceway to the parlor, they surveyed the room with a look of amused dignity. McCluskie swept off his hat and made a game try at what passed for a bow.

"Ladies, we bring you greetings." Straightening, he gestured toward the boy, who was propped up against the doorjamb. "This here is Mr. Kinch Riley, sportin' man supreme."

Everything in the room came to a stop. Belle, along with three cowhands and five girls, stared back at them as if man and boy had suddenly sprung whole from a crack in the floor. Kinch pulled his hat off and grinned like a cat with a mouthful of feathers. But he had a little trouble duplicating McCluskie's bow. All at once his joints seemed limber as goose grease and he couldn't quite manage to peel himself off the door-jamb.

Belle crossed the room and planted herself directly in their path. She looked them both up and down, shaking her head ruefully. Then she sniffed, as if one of them had broken wind, and her gaze settled on the Irishman.

"Just proud as punch, aren't you? Finally managed to get him drunk."

"Drunk?" McCluskie tucked his chin down and gave her an owlish frown. "Who?"

"Him!" Belle's finger stabbed out and Kinch jerked back, banging his head against the door frame.

McCluskie's frown changed to a sly smirk, as if he had just heard a lie so preposterous it defied belief. "Goddamn, Belle, he's sober as a judge. You better get yourself some specs."

"You really are thick, aren't you?" Her words came clipped and sharp, like spitting grease. "You big baboon, you're so drunk he looks sober. And him sick, too. Just wait till Doc Boyd gets wind of this."

"Cough syrup," Kinch muttered.

They both blinked and gave him a peculiar look. Belle shrugged, not sure she had heard right, and after a moment McCluskie bent closer. "How's that, bud?"

"Cough syrup."

"Yeah, what about it?"

"Tastes just like cough syrup."

"You mean the whiskey?"

"Just like what they gimme at the hospital."

"What them doctors gave you back in Kansas City?"

"Only better. Lots better."

McCluskie sifted it over a minute and all of a sudden the kid made perfect sense. Canting his head back, he gave Belle a crafty look. "Thick, huh? Case you hadn't noticed, he's not coughin'. Matter of fact, he hasn't since we started drinkin'. What d'ya think of that?"

"Oh, pshaw!" she informed him. "That's no excuse to take a boy out and get him drunk."

"Belle, you're startin' to sound like a mother hen. Besides which, we didn't need an excuse. This is his birthday. Or maybe you forgot."

"I didn't forget and you know it very well. But he was supposed to get his birthday present here, not soaking up rotgut in some dingy saloon."

"Well Jesus H. Christ! Whyn't you quit makin' so much noise, then, and do somethin' about it? Hell, he's been standin' here five minutes and you haven't even introduced him to the girls."

Belle started to say something, but thought better of it. She pried Kinch off the doorjamb and waltzed him out to the middle of the parlor. The girls had watched the entire flurry with mild wonder, and now, as she graced them with a dazzling smile, they sensed that something unusual was brewing.

"Girls, you've all heard me talk about Kinch. Well, tonight is his birthday and he's come to spend it with us. Whatever he wants is on the house, so whoever gets picked, make sure he has a good time."

Nothing about her smile changed, but something in her eyes did. "Understand?"

The girls got the message. They dropped the three cowhands like so many hot rocks and came swarming over the kid. A henna-haired redhead reached him first, and wedged herself up next to his chest like a mustard plaster. Close behind came a blond with soft, jiggly breasts the size of gourds. She latched onto his other arm and started running her hand through his hair. Another blond and a mousey brunette charged into the melee, and before he had time to take a deep breath, Kinch was up to his ears in squealing females.

"Sweetie, do you like Lulu?" purred the redhead.

Kinch cast a trapped look back over his shoulder at the Irishman. But he got no sympathy there. McCluskie and Belle were going at it hammer and tongs. Evidently their little spat had only just started.

The blond stuck her melons under his nose and whispered a blast of hot air into his ear. "Ditch these others, honeybunch. Let Francie give you a trip around the world."

The boy felt as though he were drowning in a sea of arms and bosoms and clawing hands. Every time he struggled to the surface they dragged him under to the floor. Suddenly he pitched forward, spun completely around, and broke clear. Dazed and still somewhat numb from the whiskey he'd absorbed, he lurched away and almost plowed over the fifth girl. Drawing back, he swayed dangerously and tried to bring her into focus.

She was smaller than the others, just a little sprite of a girl. Her hair was black as tarpitch, and she had large almond eyes that stared out wistfully from a kewpie-doll face. Just at that moment he thought she was the most beautiful creature he'd ever seen. More importantly, if it came down to it, he thought he could

whip her in a fair fight. The others he wasn't too sure
about.

"Hi." Her mouth dimpled in a smile. "I'm Sugartit."

That threw him off stride and for an instant he
couldn't get his jaws working. Then he felt the pack
closing in behind him and he grabbed her hand.

"Let's go!"

Kinch didn't know where they were going, but
right about then his choices seemed pretty limited. He
reeled forward, head spinning crazily, aware of nothing but the girl before him.

Sugartit clutched his hand and took off toward the
rear of the parlor. The thing he always remembered
most afterward was her laugh as they went through
the door.

It was like the patter of rain on a warm spring
night.

NINE

Kinch was having a hard time looking at the girl. But toning his shirt, he kept sneaking peeks at her out of the corner of his eye. If she noticed, she didn't say anything, but he found nothing unusual in that. Anybody with a name like hers was probably used to being stared at. Maybe even liked it.

Watching her dress gave him a strange sensation down around his bellybutton. It was almost as if he could see straight through her clothes. The way she'd been in bed, soft and naked and cuddly warm. All of which was in his mind's eye, of course. He kept telling himself that as his hands fumbled with the shirt buttons. But it made the image in his head no less real.

What he saw wasn't so much the girl as the sum of her parts. Brief flashes that came and went, like lightning bugs in a dark room. Her impish smile and those big, waifish eyes. The delicate buttercup of her breasts. The gentle swell of her hips. And most of all, somehow flickering brighter than the rest, the soft black muff between her legs. That came strong and clear, sharply in focus.

It was something he would never forget. The warmth and pulsating throb and pleasure so sweet it became almost pain.

What he felt just then was so distinct and real that his mind turned inward, living it over again. Suddenly something touched him and a shiver rippled along his spine. He blinked, awareness returning in fits and starts, much as a dream fades into wakefulness. Then, all in a rush, he saw Sugartit standing before him. She was buttoning his shirt, her mouth dimpled with that small enigmatic smile.

His hands were motionless, frozen somehow to his shirtfront, just where they were before his mind wandered off. All at once he felt green as grass, clumsy and very foolish, and he quickly lowered his hands.

Sugartit finished the buttoning and began tucking his shirt into the waistband of his trousers. He just stood there watching her, gripped by a sensation so acute he couldn't put a name to it. Goosebumps popped out on his skin and a static charge brought tingly little prickles to every nerve in his body. Curiously, he was overcome by a feeling of utter helplessness. As if this mere slip of a girl, through some witchery he failed to comprehend, had cast a spell and turned him into a bumbling jackass incapable of the simplest thought.

The girl ran her arms around his waist and pressed herself close to his chest. He could feel the taut little nipples of her breasts through his shirt, and his mouth suddenly went thick and pasty. Mechanically, like some wooden Indian come to life, he put his arms around her. He felt light in the head, queer somehow, as if he were standing off in a corner watching it happen to someone else.

"There's sure not much of you." Sugartit ran her fingers over his ribs like a piano player testing chords. "You're just all bone and gristle, aren't you?"

Kinch swallowed a wad of paste. "I guess."

"Well, don't worry about it, lover." Her head arched back and the almond eyes seemed to soak him up in great gulps. "Maybe you got shortchanged on muscle, but you're all bearcat where it counts."

Suddenly he felt about eight feet tall. "You ain't exactly tame yourself."

She laughed softly and snuggled closer. "Did you like it?"

"Better'n a duck likes water." Curiously, his tongue had come unglued and he felt slick as a street-corner pitchman. "What about you?"

"Silly, of course I did. Couldn't you tell?" She gave him a tight little squeeze. "I've had it lots of ways, but never like that. Not even once."

The scent of her hair was like perfume and for an instant he couldn't get his breath. "You're joshin' me."

Sugartit put her arms around his neck and pulled his head down. Her lips came over his mouth, soft and warm, and her pink little tongue started doing tricks. Then her hips moved, undulating and hungry, and a jolt of lightning hit him just below the belt buckle. She pulled back and searched his face with a devilish smile.

"Still think I'm joshing?"

Kinch bent and lifted her in his arms. She was

surprisingly light, and it pleased him that he could heft her so easily. As he carried her toward the bed, Sugartit laughed that soft laugh again and began nibbling on his ear.

When they entered the parlor some time later everything was back to normal. Belle and the Irishman were wedged into a settee like a couple of lovebirds, and from the looks they were giving one another, it was clear that a truce of some sort had been negotiated. The girls had themselves a fresh batch of Texans, and they were paired off around the room making sweet talk. Everybody knew that this was what made Belle's prices so stiff, all the sugar and spice that came beforehand. But the cowhands didn't seem to mind in the least. They were lapping it up as fast as the girls could dish it out.

So far as the kid could see, it was business as usual.

McCluskie spotted him first and gave Belle the high sign with a jerk of his head. She looked around and then they both stood up, waiting for Sugartit and Kinch to cross the room. Belle whispered something and the Irishman smiled, but oddly enough, they had the look of expectant parents. Almost as if they were awaiting news of a blessed event.

"Bud, I'd just about given you up for lost," McCluskie grinned and tried to make it sound offhand. "Enjoy yourself, did you?"

Kinch flushed despite himself. "Yeah, sure. Best birthday I ever had."

The girl giggled and Belle eyed her speculatively.

"Sugartit, I hope you showed our young friend a good time."

. "Why, Belle, I just put the frosting on his cake. I taught him the French twist, and the half-and-half, and—"

"Whoa, Nellie!" McCluskie threw up his hand. "All that racy talk is liable to give an old man like me dangerous notions. C'mon, sport. Let's go get ourselves a drink. After a workout like that I've got an idea you need fortifyin'." He dropped an arm over the kid's shoulders and headed for the door. "Belle, I'll see you later. And if I don't, you'll know ol' hollow-leg here had put me under the table."

"Mike McCluskie, you remember what I said! Don't you dare get that boy drunk again. I'll hear about it if you do."

McCluskie laughed and kept on walking. The boy darted a look over his shoulder as he was being hustled into the hallway, and Sugartit gave him a bright smile.

"Come back soon, lover. Don't forget, you hear?"

Kinch's disembodied voice floated back through the parlor entrance. "I will. First thing tomorrow."

Then the door slammed and Belle shot the girl a funny look. Sugartit sighed and dimpled her cheeks in a pensive little frown, wondering if he really meant it.

Outside, McCluskie headed the boy uptown and they walked along at a steady clip for a few paces. After a while the Irishman grunted and shook his head.

"Let that be a lesson to you, bud. Don't ever let women get started runnin' their gums. Once they build up a head of steam, there's no stoppin' them. I got us out of there just in time."

Kinch gave him a quizzical glance. "I don't get you. What's wrong with talkin'?"

"Talkin'? Hell, there wouldn't be no talkin' to it. Just listenin'. They'd sit there and rehash the whole night, and feed it back to you blow by blow. Time they got through you'd come away thinkin' you'd lived it twice."

"Yeah, I guess I see what you mean."

They walked along in silence for a few steps, but McCluskie's curiosity finally got the better of him. Not unlike the temptation to peep through a knothole, there was a question he just couldn't resist.

"What'd you think of Sugartit?"

"She's nifty, Mike. Cuter'n a button, too."

Something in the kid's voice sounded peculiar. Just a little off key. "Well, I didn't mean her, exactly. I was talkin' about what she did for you. How'd you like that?"

Kinch didn't say anything for a moment, but an odd look came over his eyes. "It was like a big juicy toothache that don't hurt no more. All of a sudden *whammo!* And then it's fixed."

"Yeah?" McCluskie detected something more than mere excitement. "Tell me about it."

"Well, I don't know. It was like colored lights whirlin' around inside your head. Y'know, the way a skyrocket does. There's a big explosion and then for a while you can't see nothin' but streaks and colors and bright flashes. Cripes, she was somethin', Mike."

"I'm startin' to get a hunch you were drunker'n I thought."

"No I wasn't, neither. After the first time I was sober as all get out."

"First time!"

The boy grinned sheepishly. "Yeah. Y'see, we was gettin' dressed and then she started rubbin' around on me and—"

"I get the picture. What you're sayin' is that you liked it more'n you thought."

"I liked her. There's somethin' about her, Mike. She's not like the others. Not even a little bit."

The Irishman slammed to a halt and faced him. "Say, you're not gettin' sweet on that girl, are you?"

"I might be." Kinch stuck out his chin and stared right back. "What's wrong with that?"

McCluskie had seen lots of men go dippy over whores. In a cowtown there was always a scarcity of women, and sometimes a man settled for what he could get. But the kid deserved better than that. The only thing special about Sugartit was that she had probably laid half the cowhands in Texas. And her hardly older than the kid, for Chrissakes!

"What's wrong is that she's a whore. Has been since Belle stole her away from a dancehall back in Abilene. That was close to three years ago. You got any idea how many men she's screwed in —"

"Mike, I ain't gonna listen to that. Don't you go badmouthin' her, y'hear me!"

The boy was bristled up like a banty rooster and McCluskie had to clamp down hard to keep from laughing. "Don't get your dander up, bud. I was just tryin' to show you what's what."

"Well, lay off of her. I told you, she's not like the others."

"Awright, just for the sake of argument, let's say she's not. But what do you think she's doin' back there right now?"

"What kind of crack is that?"

"You think about it for a minute. She's not workin' in a sporting house for her health, y'know. There's cowhands walkin' in there regular as clockwork, and before the night's over she'll have humped her share."

Kinch glared at him for a long time, then he shrugged and looked away. "Nobody's perfect. She was probably starvin' and plenty hard up when Belle took her in."

"That's right, she was."

"Same as me, the night you caught me down at the depot."

"Not just exactly. That's what I'm tryin' to get through your head. Call her whatever you want: Soiled Dove. Fallen Sparrow. The handle you put on her won't change nothin'. The plain fact of the matter is, she's a whore."

"Well, holy jumpin' Jesus, that ain't no crime, is it? Cripes, if I was a girl and got stuck in a cowtown, I might've wound up a whore myself."

"All I'm sayin' is that you shouldn't get calf eyes over your first piece of tail. There's lots of women around. Some of 'em better'n Sugartit, maybe. You ought to shop around a little before you let yourself get all bogged down."

"I don't see you makin' the rounds. Seems to me you stick pretty close to Belle."

The kid halfway had a point. McCluskie grunted and turned back uptown. They clomped along without saying much, each lost in his own thoughts. At last, somewhat baffled by the youngster's doggedness, the Irishman decided to try another tack.

"Y'know, it's funny how things work out between a man and a woman. Now you take Belle and me, for instance. Once I get her in bed she's tame as any tabbycat you ever saw. But the rest of the time she's got a temper that'd melt lead. Hell, I don't need to tell you. Not after some of the tantrums you've seen her pitch."

Kinch gave him a suspicious look. "What's that got to do with me and Sugartit?"

"That's what I was workin' around to. You see, it's like this: When a man's puttin' the goods to a woman, she's putty in his hands. There's not a promise on earth she wouldn't make while he's got his shaft ticklin' her funnybone. But out of bed it's a different story. Then she knows he's got his mind on the next time, and that gives her the whiphand. She'll make him sweat and do all kinds of damnfool things before she lets him climb in the saddle again."

"I still don't see what that's got to do with anything."

"You're not listenin', bud. What I'm sayin' is that women calculate things. Plan it all out. A man's brains are between his legs, and that's where he does most of his thinkin'. A woman thinks with her head, leastways when you haven't got her on her back, and she generally winds up gettin' what she wants."

"What you're sayin' is that women know how to wind a man around their little finger."

"That's exactly what I'm sayin'. Just remember, a man rules in bed, but the rest of the time it's the woman that calls the tune. They'll make you dance

whatever jig they want just for the honor of pumpin'
on 'em every now and then."

"And you think that's what Sugartit has got
planned for me?"

"She's female, and I'm just tellin' you that's the
way they work."

Kinch screwed up his face in a stubborn frown.
"Mike, that's the biggest crock I ever heard. Maybe
I'm wet behind the ears, but I'm not stupid. Sugartit
is different, and nothin' you say is gonna budge me
one iota."

It suddenly dawned on McCluskie that he was up
against a stone wall. Not only that, but he was trying
to play God in the bargain. Here was a kid who'd be
lucky if he lived out the winter, and the last thing he
needed was a bunch of second-hand advice—especially from somebody who hadn't made any great
shakes of his own life. If the kid wanted a playmate
till his string ran out, then by damn that's what he
would have. Sugartit was handy and seemed willing,
so it was just a matter of working it out with Belle.
The button wouldn't even have to know.

McCluskie threw his arm over the boy's shoulders.
"Sport, I learned a long time ago not to argue with a
man when he's got his mind set. Besides, maybe you
know something I don't. Hell, give it a whirl. You
and Sugartit might hit it off in style. Just remember
what I said, though. Keep your dauber up and she'll
treat you like Jesus H. himself."

The kid grinned and started to reply, but all at once
his throat constricted and he began coughing. It
wasn't a particularly severe spasm but it was the
worst of the night. Watching him gasp for air, the

Irishman was again reminded of his promise to himself. This kid was going to have whatever he wanted. Served up any way he liked.

"Goddamn, I knew it!" McCluskie growled. "You sobered up and now you're back to coughin'. C'mon, bud, what you need is a drink. Let's find ourselves a waterin' hole."

They crossed the street and entered Gregory's Saloon. This was a Texan hangout and a place McCluskie normally wouldn't have frequented, but just then he wasn't feeling choosy. Whiskey was whiskey, and the kid needed a dose in the worst way.

The dive was packed shoulder to shoulder with trailhands, and reeked of sweat, cow manure, and stale smoke. McCluskie bulled his way through the crowd and wedged out a place for them at the bar. Some of the men he shoved aside muttered angrily, and a curious buzz swept back over the room as others turned to look at the choking, red-faced kid.

The bartender sauntered over, absently munching a toothpick. "What'll you have?"

"The good stuff," McCluskie informed him. "With the live snake in it."

That didn't draw any laughs but it produced a bottle. The Irishman poured and got a shot down Kinch without any lost motion. Apparently even snakehead whiskey was not without medicinal qualities. It had no sooner hit bottom than the kid stopped coughing and commenced to look like himself again. McCluskie poured a second round just for good measure.

"Say, Irish, when'd ya start collectin' strays?"

Several of the men close by chuckled, and McCluskie turned to find Bill Bailey standing a few feet behind him. They had crossed paths back in Abilene and shared a mutual dislike for one another. Bailey was a big man, heavier than McCluskie, with a seamed, windburned face the color of plug tobacco. His legs bowed out like a couple of barrel staves, and it was no secret that he had once been a top hand for Shanghai Pierce. According to rumor, he had a checkered past and couldn't return to Texas—something about a shootout over a card game that had left a reward dodger hanging over his head. But he was a great favorite with the trailhands, and through one device or another, managed to leave them laughing, as he separated them from their pay.

McCluskie gave him a brittle stare. "Bailey, I only allow my friends to call me Irish. That lets you out."

"Hell, don't get your nose out of joint." Bailey jerked a thumb at Kinch. "I was just curious about your pardner. Looks a mite sickly to be runnin' with you."

"Don't let his looks fool you." McCluskie turned his head slightly and winked at the kid. "For a skinny fellow he's sorta sudden."

Bailey cocked one eyebrow and inspected the boy closer. "Yeh, that popgun he's wearin' looks real, sure enough. Course, I've seen more'n one pilgrim shoot his toes off tryin' to play badman. What about it, squirt, you lost any toes lately?"

McCluskie leaned back against the bar and studied the ceiling. The kid glanced at him and got no reaction whatever. Then it came to him, what was happening here, and a smile ticked at the corner of his mouth.

The Irishman had slyly brought the game full circle.

Kinch turned his attention back to the Texan. "Mister, that's a bad habit you've got, callin' people names. Some folks might not take kindly to it."

Bailey's eyes narrowed and he darted a puzzled look at the Irishman. "Listen, sonny, my beef's with your friend here. Just button your lip and I'll act like I didn't hear you."

All at once the kid knew what McCluskie had been talking about every day out in the gully: the difference between a tin can and a man. It brought a warm little glow down in the pit of his belly.

"What's the matter, lardgut? Lost your nerve?"

"Boy, I'm warnin' you, don't rile me. You're out of your class."

It was just like McCluskie had said! A four-flusher always toots his horn the loudest. He smiled and edged clear of the bar.

"Try me."

Bailey's hand twitched and streaked toward the butt of his gun. Then he froze dead still. The kid was standing there with a Colt Navy pointed straight at his gut. What the Texan took to be his last thought was one of sheer wonder. He hadn't even seen the kid move.

McCluskie waited a couple of seconds, then looked over at the boy. "You figure on shootin' him?"

Kinch shook his head. "Nope, He's not worth it."

McCluskie shrugged and headed toward the door. The boy backed away, keeping Bailey covered, and only after he was outside did he holster the Colt. The Irishman was already striding up the street, and as

Kinch came alongside he grunted sourly.

"That was a damnfool play. A gun's like what you've got between your legs. If you're not going to use it, then keep it in your pants. Saves a whole lot of trouble later on."

TEN

The five men were seated around a table in the Lone Star. They were alone, for sunrise was scarcely an hour past, and none of the saloon help had yet arrived. Spivey and Judge Muse, flanked by Tonk Hazeltine, occupied one side of the table. Seated across from them were McCluskie and Bill Bailey.

Not unlike dogs warily eying one another, the Texan and McCluskie had their chairs hitched around sideways to the table. They had exchanged curt nods when the meeting began, and afterward seated themselves so they could keep each other in sight. This guarded maneuvering was hardly lost on the others, yet none of them displayed any real surprise. The story of Bailey's humiliation at the hands of the kid was by now common knowledge. It had created a sensation on both sides of the tracks, and except for the upcoming bond issue, the townspeople had talked of little else for the last week.

Word had spread that Bailey meant to even the score, and hardly anyone doubted he would try. Unless McCluskie got to him first, which seemed highly likely. Still, betting was about evenly split, and speculation was widespread as to the outcome if it ever came to a showdown.

When the men first sat down, Spivey had attempted to ease the tension with some idle chitchat. But it quickly became apparent that his efforts were largely wasted. While Muse joined in, the others simply stared back at him like a flock of molting owls. Hazeltine and Bailey shared a bitter dislike for the Irishman, who in turn, looked through them as if they didn't exist. Spivey finally gave it up as hopeless and at last got down to business.

"Gents, I called this meetin' so we could get everything squared away neat and proper. Once the votin' commences I don't figure we're gonna have much chance to get our heads together. Whatever's got to be ironed out, we'd best get to it now. Later we likely won't have time."

There was a moment of silence while everybody digested that. After a while Hazeltine cleared his throat. "I don't follow you. What's left to be done?"

"Well, Tonk, when we agreed to deputize these boys"—Spivey waved his hand in the general direction of McCluskie and Bailey—"we sort of thought you'd make good use of 'em. I kept waitin' but as of last night you hadn't said yea or nay. Seemed to me we oughta talk about it."

"What's to talk about?" The lawman gave him an indignant frown. "I'm the law here and I'll see that everything comes off the way it's s'posed to."

Spivey and Muse exchanged glances. Then the judge made a steeple of his fingers and peered through them at Hazeltine. "Deputy, we're not casting aspersions on you personally. Nothing of the sort. We're merely asking what your plans are."

"Hell, we don't need no plans. You talk like we was electin' a new President or somethin'. It's nothin' but a measly goddamn bond vote."

Spivey swelled up like a bloated toad. "Measly, my dusty rump! Just in case it slipped your mind, what happens today could put the quietus on this whole town. What's at stake here is Newton itself."

"Bob's right," the judge agreed hurriedly. "We're fighting for our lives. Now let me tell you something. Six months ago this town was nothing but a cow pasture. Today we have a bank, hotels, businesses. A thriving economy. And something more, too. The potential—"

McCluskie turned a deaf ear to the judge's harangue. The past month had left him with a sour taste in his mouth for the grubby little game being played out here. Wichita was trying to shaft Newton. The Santa Fe was shafting everybody. And he was caught squarely in the middle.

All because the head office brass wanted to squeeze a lousy two hundred thousand dollars out of Sedgwick County.

But then, that's how the rich got fat and the poor got lean. The big dog kept nibbling away, bit by bit, at the little dog's bone. Which didn't concern him one way or the other. Except that the brass acted like they had a case of the trots and couldn't find the plug.

They had ordered him to split Newton down the middle and that's what he'd done. Pony Reid and John Gallagher started talking it up and before long the sporting crowd had swung over to Wichita's side of the fence. All of which made good sense from their standpoint. Wichita was farther south than any of the cowtowns and was sure to attract a greater number of the Texas herds.

Then, out of a clear blue, the brass told him to lay off. They had decided, according to their last letter, to let Sedgwick County resolve its own internal affairs. Stripped of all subterfuge, it simply meant they intended to play both ends against the middle. Whoever won—Newton or Wichita—the Santa Fe would still wind up with all the marbles.

If it wasn't so infuriating he might have laughed. The fact that they paid him to waste his time and effort only made it more absurd. Like a dog chasing its tail, he had accomplished nothing.

Judge Muse brought him back to the present with a sharp rap on the table. "We're fighting for nothing less than our very lives! Everything we possess has been poured into this town. Speaking quite frankly, Deputy, I think that demands some added effort on your part also."

Tonk Hazeltine gave him a glum scowl. "I already said my piece. Trouble with you fellers is you're makin' a mountain out of a molehill."

"Like hell we are!" Spivey replied hotly. "This town'll be swamped with Texans today, and if I know them they won't miss a chance to hooraw things good and proper. It's our election, but odds are they'll use it as an excuse to pull Newton up by the roots."

"Which could disrupt the voting," Muse added, "and easily jeopardize whatever chance we have of defeating the bond issue."

Hazeltine said nothing, merely staring back at them. Spivey and the judge looked nonplused, but it was all the Irishman could do to keep from grinning. What he had suspected from the outset was now quite apparent. The lawman was all bluff, and he plainly wasn't overjoyed by the prospect of cracking down on the cowhands. Muse and Spivey had blinded themselves to the truth, staking their hopes on his much publicized reputation. Right now he was the only law the town had, and they couldn't see past the glitter of his tin star.

The silence thickened and after a moment Spivey glanced over at the Irishman. "What d'ya think, Mike? Isn't there some way we could keep the lid on till after the votin' is done with?"

"Why the hell you askin' him?" Bailey snarled. "The only thing he ever give Texans was a hard time, and you'd better believe they ain't forgot it neither."

Judge Muse raised his hand in a curbing gesture. "Mr. Bailey, may I remind you that you and Mr. McCluskie were deputized in an effort to even things out. You're a Texan, and you should be able to reason with them if things get out of hand. Mr. McCluskie, on the other hand, is versed in—shall we say, keeping the peace—and that, too, has its place. All things considered, it seems like a good combination."

"Like hell!" Bailey rasped, edging forward in his chair. "You turn him loose with a badge and I guaran-damn-tee you there's gonna be trouble. He's got it in for Texans and everybody knows it."

McCluskie pulled out the makings and started building a smoke. "There's only one Texan I'm on the lookout for, and you're sittin' in his chair."

"You're gonna get it sooner'n you think." Bailey half rose to his feet, then thought better of it and hastily sat down. "That goes for your snot-nosed side-kick, too."

The Irishman fired up his cigarette and took a deep drag. Then he tossed the match aside and smiled, exhaling smoke. "Bailey, you monkey with me and I'll put a leak in your ticker. Any time you think different, you just try me."

Spivey broke in before the Texan could frame an answer. "Now everybody just simmer down. Whatever personal grudge you've got is between you two. But for God's sake, let's keep the peace today. C'mon now, what d'ya say? Do I have your word on that—both of you?"

When neither man responded, the saloonkeeper hurried on as though it were all settled. "Good. Now, Mike, you never did answer my question. What do we do to keep the lid on?"

McCluskie puffed thoughtfully on his cigarette. "Where's the votin' booth? Horner's Store, isn't it?"

"That's right. What with it bein' just north of the tracks, we figured it was handy to everybody concerned."

"Yeah, that sounds reasonable." The Irishman took a swipe at his mustache, mulling some thought a moment longer. "Way I see it, the thing to do is to keep the cowhands from crossin' the tracks in any big bunches. Hazeltine could watch over Horner's, and me and Bailey could patrol opposite sides of the street down on the southside. That way if any trouble starts we could close in on it from three sides. Oughtn't to be that much of a problem if we handle it right."

Hazeltine stiffened in his chair and glared around at Spivey. "Who's callin' the shots here, me or him?"

McCluskie chuckled and flipped his cigarette in the direction of a spittoon. "Tonk, the man just asked for some advice. I wouldn't have the job on a bet."

Spivey nodded vigorously, looking from one to the other. "Course, you're callin' the shots, Tonk. Wouldn't have it any other way. But you'll have to admit, he's got a pretty good idea."

The deputy pursed his lips and shrugged with a great show of reluctance. "Yeah, I guess so. Probably wouldn't hurt none for me to stick close to that votin' booth."

McCluskie wiped his mouth to hide a grin. *Wouldn't hurt none.* What a joke! The sorry devil had been oozing sweat at the thought of patrolling the southside. Holed up in Horner's was just his speed. Likely what he had intended doing all along.

Judge Muse climbed to his feet, smiling affably. "Then it's all settled. Gentlemen, I'm happy to see we've reached an accord. I, for one, have a feeling this is going to be a red-letter day in the history of Newton."

The men pushed out of their chairs, standing, and Bailey's gut gave off a thunderous rumble. Someone suggested breakfast and the others quickly agreed. Despite Randolph Muse's optimistic forecast, they shared a hunch that it wasn't a day to be faced on an empty stomach.

Walking back to the hotel, McCluskie couldn't shake an edgy feeling about Bailey. The man was a loudmouth and a bully, but he was no coward. Not that he wouldn't backshoot somebody if that seemed the best way. He would and probably had. Yet even that took a certain amount of sand, and Bailey had his share.

The Irishman wasn't worried about himself. Characters like Bailey were strictly penny-ante, and there was a certain savor in beating them at their own game. But the threat against the kid was another matter altogether. It was very real, and Bailey had ample reason to want the youngster dead. Making a fool of a hardcase, who had set himself up as bull-of-the-woods, was a risky sport. It could get a man—or a boy—gunned down in a dark alley. Or in bed. Or just about any place where he least expected it.

Thinking of the kid made him chuckle, but it was amusement heavily larded with concern. These days the button was cocky as a young rooster. That he had shaded Bailey on the draw was only part of it. Mostly it had to do with a girl named Sugar, and the fact that she had become his regular girl. Not that she was his alone, but she came as close as she could. Sugar was one of Belle's girls, and Belle was a businesswoman first and last, and even for the kid her generosity had certain limits. After listening to McCluskie's arguments she had agreed to a compromise of sorts. Sugar could see the kid all she wanted on her off time, and so long as he made a definite appointment at night, Belle wouldn't use the girl for the parlor trade. Otherwise Sugar would work the same as usual, which meant that she was the boy's private stock, but only about halfway.

The kid wasn't exactly overjoyed by the arrangement, yet he couldn't help but strut his stuff the least little bit. Sugar had a knack about her, there was no denying that. She had convinced him that he was the only real man in her life, and every time they were together, he came away fairly prancing. What they had wasn't just the way he wanted it, but it was far more than he'd ever had before. Life had dealt him enough low blows so that having Sugar, even on a part-time basis, seemed like a stroke of luck all done up in a fancy ribbon. The way he talked it was as if the bitter and the sweet had finally equaled out. He was happy as a pig in mud, only he couldn't stop wishing the wallow was his alone.

When McCluskie entered the room, he found the kid standing before the mirror, practicing his draw. Every day the boy got a shade faster, but smooth along with it, as though somebody had slapped a liberal dose of grease on a streak of chain-lightning. The Irishman felt a little like God, profoundly awed at what he had wrought.

Kinch saw him in the mirror and turned, holstering the Colt in one slick motion. "Just practicin' a little. I been waitin' breakfast for you."

"Already had mine." McCluskie cocked his thumb and forefinger and gestured at the pistol. "You've got yourself honed down to a pretty fine edge. What's the sense if you won't shoot nothin' but tin cans?"

"Same song, second verse. You're talkin' about Bailey again, aren't you?"

"That'll do for openers."

"Mike, I done told you fifty zillion times. I had him cold. There wasn't no need to shoot him. He was froze tighter'n an icicle."

"There's some men that would've dusted you on both sides while you was standin' there admirin' how fast you were. You try pullin' a fool stunt like that again and the jasper you're facin' might just be the one that proves it to you."

"Okay, professor." The kid smiled and threw up his hands to ward off the lecture. "You don't have to keep beatin' me over the head with it. I got the idea."

"Yeah, but have you got the stomach for it? I've been tellin' you not to wear that gun unless you mean to use it next time. So far you've given me a lot of talk but you haven't said anything."

"Awright, I'm sayin' it. Next time I won't hold off."

McCluskie eyed him skeptically. "Sometimes I think it was a mistake to give you that gun. Might have saved us all a pile of grief."

"You lost me. Where's the grief in me packin' a gun?"

"I just came from a meetin' with the big nabobs." The Irishman hesitated, turning it over in his head, and decided there was nothing to be gained in holding back. "Bailey was there and he started makin' noises about nailin' you. Course, he's been makin' the same brag all over town, so it's not exactly news. But it's past the talkin' stage now. He'll have to make his play soon."

"Aren't you and him gonna be workin' together today?"

"Now what's that got to do with the price of tea?"

"Nothin'. I was just thinkin' I might tag along with you."

McCluskie grunted, shaking his head. "Bud, you're barking up the wrong tree. Bailey knows better than to mess with me. It's you he's after."

"Still wouldn't do no harm."

"Maybe. But we'll never find out. I want you to stick close to the room today. I'll have the cafe send up your meals."

"Aw, cripes a'mighty, Mike. I'm not a kid no more. If he's spoilin' for a fight it might as well be sooner as later."

The Irishman studied him a moment, weighing the alternatives. "No soap. I'll sic you on him when I'm convinced you won't hold off pullin' the trigger. Meantime, you keep your butt in this room. Savvy?"

Kinch spun away and kicked a chair halfway across the room. "Horseapples!"

McCluskie walked to the door, then turned and glanced back. "How's your cough today?"

The kid wouldn't look at him. "Why, you writin' a book or somethin'?"

"Keep your dauber up, sport. There's better days ahead."

The door closed softly behind him and an oppressive silence fell over the room. Kinch flung himself down on the bed and just lay there, staring at the ceiling. Then he felt the first tingle deep down in his throat.

He waited, knotting his fists, wondering what his lungs would spew up this morning.

Shortly after the noon hour Hugh Anderson and his crew rode into town. McCluskie saw them pull up and dismount before the Red Front Saloon, and his scalp went prickly all of a sudden. That explained it. Why things had been so quiet all morning. The Texans crowding the saloons up and down the street had been biding their time. Waiting for the big dog himself to start the show.

Anderson and his hands were the bane of every cowtown in Kansas. They were wild and loud, rambunctious in the way of overgrown boys testing their manhood. Only their pranks sometimes got out of hand, and they had a tendency to see how far a town could be pushed before it stood up and fought back. Their leader was an arrogant young smart aleck, the son of a Texas cattle baron, and he had developed quite a reputation for devising new ways to hooraw Kansas railheads. Worse yet, he fancied himself as something of a gunslinger, and had an absolute gift for provoking senseless shootouts.

McCluskie knew what was coming and headed toward the tracks at a fast clip. Crossing Fourth, he scanned the street for Bailey, meaning to give him the high sign, but the Texan was nowhere in sight. Before he could reach the next corner, men began boiling out of saloons and Anderson's crew was quickly joined by another forty or fifty cowhands. There was considerable shouting and arm waving, and suddenly the crowd split and everybody raced for their horses. The Irishman jerked his pistol and took off at a dead run.

But he was no match for them afoot, and they thundered across the tracks even as he passed the hotel. Townspeople were lined up outside Horner's Store waiting to vote and the Texans barreled down on them like a band of howling Indians. Anderson opened fire first, splintering the sign over the bank, and within moments it sounded as if a full scale war had broken out. Glass shattered, lead whanged through the high false-front structures overhead, and above it all came the shrill Rebel yells of Texans on the rampage.

Most of the town had gathered to watch the balloting, and now they stampeded before the cowhands like scalded dogs. Women clutched their children and ran screaming along the street, while men scattered and leaped into nearby doorways seeking shelter. The Texans made a clean sweep up North Main, laughing and whooping and drilling holes through anything that even faintly resembled a target. Then they whirled their ponies and came charging back toward the tracks.

Tonk Hazeltine made the mistake of stepping out of Horner's Store just at that moment. Had he remained inside the cowhands would probably have kept on going, satisfied that they had taught the Yankee bloodsuckers a lesson. But the sight of a tin star was a temptation too great to resist.

Hugh Anderson skidded his horse to a halt, and the Texans reined in behind him, cloaked in a billowing cloud of dust. Hazeltine stood his ground on the boardwalk, watching and saying nothing as they walked their horses toward him. When they stopped, Anderson hooked one leg over his saddlehorn and grinned, gesturing toward the deputy.

"Well now, looka here what we caught ourselves, boys. A real live peace officer. Shiny badge and all."

The Texans thought it a rare joke and burst out in fits of laughter. Circling around behind them, McCluskie saw the lawman's face redden but couldn't tell if he said anything or not. It occurred to him that Hazeltine was probably too scared to draw his gun. Still, if he could just get the drop on them from behind it might shake the deputy out of his funk. Once they had the cowhands covered front and rear that would most likely put an end to it.

McCluskie raised his pistol but all at once cold steel jabbed him in the back of the neck. With it came the metallic whirr of a hammer being thumbed back and a grated command.

"Unload it, Irish! Otherwise I'll scatter your brains all over Kingdom Come."

One of McCluskie's cardinal rules was that a man never argued with a gun at his head. Slowly, keeping his hand well in sight, he lowered the Colt and dropped it in the street. Then he stood very still.

There was no need to look around. Bill Bailey's voice was one in a hundred. Maybe even a thousand.

With or without a cocked pistol.

ELEVEN

~~~~~~~

Bailey marched the Irishman forward, nudging him in the backbone every couple of steps with the pistol. The cowhands' attention was distracted from Hazeltine for a moment, and they turned in their saddles to watch this curious little procession. McCluskie looked straight ahead, ignoring their stares, and took his lead from the jabs in his spine. They circled around the skittish ponies and came to a halt before Hugh Anderson.

"What've you got there, Billy?" Anderson was casually rolling himself a smoke. "Another lawdog?"

"He's the one I told you about. Pride and joy of the Santee Fe. Ain't you, Irish?"

McCluskie kept his mouth shut, coolly inspecting Anderson. The Texan was older than he expected. Pushing thirty, with a bulge around his beltline that spoke well of beans and sowbelly and rotgut whiskey. A hard drinker, clearly a man with a taste for the fast life. But for all the lard he was packing, there was nothing soft about him. His face looked like it had

been carved out of seasoned hickory, and back deep
in his eyes there was a peculiar glint, feverish and
piercing.

All of a sudden McCluskie decided to play it very
loose. He had seen that look before. Cold and inscru-
table, but alert. The look of a man who enjoyed dous-
ing cats with coal oil just to watch them burn.

"McCluskie." The word came out flat and toneless.
Anderson flicked a sulphurhead across his saddlehorn
and lit the cigarette.

"You're the one that had everybody walkin' on
eggshells back in Abilene."

"Yeah, that's him," Bailey crowed. "The big tough
Mick. Leastways he thinks he is."

"Bailey, whatever I am," McCluskie observed
softly, "I don't switch sides in the middle of a fight."

"He's got you there, Billy." Anderson smiled but
there was no humor in his eyes. "Folks hereabouts are
gonna start callin' you a turncoat, sure as hell."

"No such thing," Bailey declared hotly. "I just
played along, that's all. So's you boys would get the
lowdown."

He rammed McCluskie in the spine with the gun
barrel. "You smart-mouth sonovabitch, I oughta fix
your wagon right now."

Anderson laughed, thoroughly enjoying himself.
"Hold off there, Billy. We can't have people sayin'
we go around murderin' folks. Besides, I got a better
idea." His gaze settled on McCluskie and the odd
light flickered a little brighter. "You. Trot it on over
there beside jellyguts."

The Irishman's expression betrayed nothing. He
walked forward, mounted the boardwalk, and took a

position alongside Hazeltine. The deputy shot him a nervous glance, but just then he couldn't be bothered. His attention was focused on Anderson.

The Texans were also watching their leader, not quite sure what he had in mind. But knowing him, there was unspoken agreement that it was certain to be a real gutbuster. Whatever it was.

Anderson just sat there, leg hooked over the saddlehorn, puffing clouds of smoke as he contemplated the lawmen. People appeared from buildings along the street and started edging closer, drawn in some perverse way to the silent struggle taking place in front of Horner's Store. At last Anderson smiled, nodding to himself, and flipped his cigarette at Hazeltine's feet.

"Let's see how fast you two can shuck out of them duds." Idly he jerked his thumb toward the southside. "We're gonna have ourselves a little race. Last one to hit the town limits gets his head shaved."

The cowhands cackled uproariously, slapping one another on the back as they marveled at the sheer artistry of it. Goddamn if Hughie hadn't done it again, they shouted back and forth. Come up with a real lalapalooza! On the whole they looked proud as punch, as if the sentence rendered by Anderson somehow reflected their own good judgment. The jeers and catcalls they directed at the lawmen made it clear that they wanted no time lost in getting the show on the road.

Hazeltine began shaking like a dog passing peach pits, and it was plain to everyone watching that he was scared out of his wits. Without his badge to hide behind, divested of even his clothes, there was no telling what these crazy Texans would do to him. He had thought to talk them back over to the southside once they'd had their fun, but it was obvious now that he would be lucky to escape with his life. The fear showed in his face, and not unlike a small child being marched to the woodshed, he started peeling off his shirt.

McCluskie just stood there.

Anderson eyed him a moment, then grinned. "Hoss, you better get to strippin'. Jellyguts there'll outrun you six ways to Sunday if you try racin' in them boots."

The Irishman met and held his gaze. "I guess I'll stand pat."

"Cousin, you don't seem to get the picture. I ain't offered you a choice. I only told you how it was gonna be. *Sabe?*"

McCluskie did something funny with his wrist and a .41 Derringer appeared in his hand, cocked and centered squarely on the Texan's chest. "Your boys might get me, but I'll pull this trigger before I go down. What d'ya say, check or bet?"

"Well now, don't that beat all? Got himself a hide-out gun." Anderson was laughing but he didn't make any sudden moves. At that range the Derringer would bore a hole the size of a silver dollar. "I got to hand it to you, cousin. You're bold as brass, damned if you ain't."

"Yeah, but I get nervous when I'm spooked. You talk much more and this popgun's liable to go off in your face."

Anderson studied him a couple of seconds, then

shrugged. "What the hell? It wouldn't have been much of a race anyhow."

"Judas Priest, Hugh!" Bailey scuttled forward, waving his pistol like a divining rod. "Don't let him back you down. He's runnin' a sandy. Can't you see that?"

"Bailey, my second shot's for you." McCluskie's voice was so low the Texans had to strain to catch his words. "Keep talkin' and you'll get an extra hole right between your eyes."

"Back off, Billy!" Anderson's command stopped Bailey dead in his tracks. "Trouble with you is you never could tell a bluff from the real article. He's holdin' the goods."

Bailey kicked at a clod of dirt and walked off. After a moment Anderson's mouth cracked in a tight smile. "McCluskie, we'll just write this off to unfinished business. There's always another day. Now, why don't you make tracks before some of my boys get itchy?"

"What about Hazeltine?" the Irishman asked.

"What about him?"

"I thought maybe I'd just take him along with me."

"Don't push your luck, cousin." Anderson scowled and the feverish glow again lighted his eyes. "Our deal don't include him."

When McCluskie hesitated, he laughed. "Mebbe you're thicker'n I thought. You got some notion of gettin' yourself killed over a two-bit marshal?"

McCluskie glanced at the lawman out of the corner of his eye, then shook his head. "Nope. Just figured it was worth a try."

"So you tried," Anderson remarked, dismissing

him with a jerk of his head. "See you in church."

The Irishman stepped off the boardwalk and backed away, keeping Anderson covered as he circled around the milling horses. Once clear, he saw Spivey and Judge Muse standing in the doorway of the Lone Star and made a beeline to join them. Both men looked grim as death warmed over, and at the sight of the Derringer in his hand they paled visibly. While they had caught only snatches of the conversation between Anderson and the Irishman, there was no need to ask questions. It was all too obvious that a killing had been averted by only the slimmest of margins. McCluskie retrieved his pistol from the street and came to stand beside them in the doorway.

Tonk Hazeltine was left the star attraction of the Texans' impromptu theatrical. Accompanied by a chorus of gibes and hooting laughter, he skinned out of his clothing a piece at a time. Shirt, gunbelt, pants, and boots hit the street in rapid succession, and at last he stood before them in nothing but his longjohns and hat. Bare to the waist, he made a ludicrous figure, like some comic scarecrow being ridiculed by a flock of birds. Half-naked, humiliated in the eyes of the townspeople, he had been stripped of much more than his clothes. The reputation he had brought to Newton was gone, vanished in an instant of shame, and with it the last vestiges of his backbone.

He stood alone and cowering, a broken man.

The Texans gave him a head start and choused him south across the tracks at a shambling lope. His hat flew off as he passed the depot and every few steps they dusted his heels with a flurry of gunshots. All along the street the sporting crowd jammed the boardwalks watching in stunned silence as his ordeal was played out to its conclusion. Never once did Hazeltine utter a sound, but his eyes were wild and terror-stricken, and tears sluiced down over his cheeks even as he ran. The last they saw of him, he was limping aimlessly across the prairie, a solitary wanderer on the road to his own private hell.

Anderson and Bailey hadn't joined in the chase. They watched from in front of Horner's Store, seemingly content to let the cowhands share whatever glory remained in the final act. Now, grinning and thoroughly delighted with themselves, they became aware of the three men standing outside the Lone Star. Anderson reined his horse about, with Bailey walking alongside, and they crossed the street. Halting a few paces off, the cattleman gave McCluskie a gloating smile, then turned his attention to Spivey and Muse.

"Gents, it would appear your little metropolis needs itself a new marshal."

Judge Muse bristled and shook his finger at the Texan. "Anderson, you've brought yourself a peck of trouble. That was a deputy sheriff you ran off, which makes this a county matter. Tomorrow at the latest the sheriff himself will be up here with a warrant for your arrest."

"Is that a fact?" Anderson studied him with mock seriousness for a moment, as if amused by the jabber of a backward child. "What would you like to bet that the sheriff don't get within ten miles of Newton?"

Bailey laughed, plainly taken with the idea. "Yeah, he ain't comin' up here to pull your fat out of the fire. Hell, we'd send him hightailin' in his drawers the same as Hazeltine."

"Which come election time," Anderson added, "might look real bad to the voters. Or don't you gents agree?"

The logic of Anderson's argument was all too persuasive. Spivey and the judge exchanged bemused glances, and in the look was admission of defeat. Whatever help there was for Newton wouldn't come from a sheriff whose bread was buttered by Wichita voters. The town was on its own, and like storm clouds gathering in a darkened sky, it was plain for all to see.

"By damn, it don't end there," Spivey declared. "We'll just hire ourselves a marshal of our own. That's what we should've done in the first place."

Anderson leaned forward, crossing his arms over the saddlehorn. "Now I'm glad you brought that up. Fact is, I was thinkin' along the same lines myself."

Muse eyed him suspiciously. "I fail to see where it concerns you."

"That's where you're wrong, judge. Case you don't know it, me and my boys have got this town treed. Just offhand, I'd say that gives us quite a voice in who gets picked as lawdog."

"By any chance," Muse sniffed, "were you thinking of nominating yourself for the job?"

"You got a sense of humor, old man. I like that." Anderson grinned and dropped his hand on Bailey's shoulder. "No, the feller I had in mind was Billy here. With him totin' that badge you'd have a townful of the friendliest bunch of Texans you ever seen."

Spivey's face purpled with rage. "I'll kiss a pig's

tail before that happens. Newton's not gonna have any back-stabbin' jackleg for a marshal."

Bailey jerked as if stung by a wasp and started forward. "Swizzleguts, I'm gonna clean your plow."

McCluskie had been standing back observing, but now he shifted away from the door. "Bailey, you're liable to start something you can't finish."

The Texan stopped short and his beady eyes narrowed in a scowl. "Big tough Mick, aren't you? Think you're fast enough to take both of us?"

McCluskie smiled, waiting. "There's one way to find out."

Anderson had seen other men smile that way. Cold and taunting, eager somehow, like a hungry cat. The odds didn't suit him and he very carefully left his arms folded over the saddlehorn. Bailey glanced around, suddenly aware that he was playing a lone hand. After a moment he grunted, ripping the deputy badge from his shirt, and flung it to the ground.

"Jam it! I got better things to do anyway."

Everybody stood there and looked at each other for a while and it was finally Anderson who broke the stalemate. "Judge, you and Spivey oughta think it over. Not go off half-cocked, if y'see what I mean. You put that tin star on anybody besides Billy and I got an idea Newton's in for hard times."

Then his gaze fell on the Irishman. "You've braced me twice today. Third time out and your number's up."

McCluskie gave him the same frozen smile. "Don't bet your life on it."

Anderson reined his horse back and rode off toward the southside. Trailing behind, Bailey ambled along like a bear with a sore paw. From the doorway of the Lone Star, the three men watched after them, and at last Spivey let out his breath between clenched teeth.

"Christ!"

Late that afternoon nine men gathered in the small backroom office of the Lone Star. Among them were saloonkeepers, businessmen, one judge, and a blacksmith. They comprised the Town Board, and their chairman, Bob Spivey, had called them into emergency session. None of them questioned why they were there, or that a crisis existed. But as they stood around the smoke-filled room staring at one another, few of the men had any real hope of solving what seemed an insoluble mess.

When the last member arrived, Spivey rapped on his desk for order and stood to face them. "Men, I'm not gonna waste time rehashin' what's happened today. Most of you saw it for yourselves, and them that didn't has heard the particulars more'n once by now. The thing is, we've got ourselves a real stemwinder of a problem, and before we leave here we're gonna have to figure out what to do about it. Otherwise you can kiss the town of Newton good-by. That goes for whatever money you've got invested here, too. Now, instead of me blabberin' on about the fix we've got ourselves in, I'm gonna throw the floor open for discussion. Who's first?"

The men looked around at one another, hesitant to take the lead, and after a moment Randolph Muse cleared his throat. Rising from his chair, he studied each face in turn, as if in the hope of discovering some chink in their stony expressions. Though he had tussled with the problem all afternoon, he had yet to settle on the best approach. They were a disparate group, with conflicting interests and loyalties, and it would be no simple matter to hammer out an accord. Not a man among them could be bullied, and logic was an equation foreign to their character. That narrowed the alternatives considerably. Leaving perhaps only one appeal which might muster some solidarity in what lay before them.

"Gentlemen, what I have to say will be short and straight to the point. Where there is no law all values disappear. Whether on life or on property. Newton was founded on a cornerstone of greed, and I think each of us is honest enough to admit that to ourselves. We came here hoping to make our fortune, and for no other reason. Unless we restore law and order to this town there is every likelihood we will leave here paupers."

He paused, screwing up his most judicious frown. "Without restraints of some sort, the Texans will turn this into one big graveyard long before you can unload your business on some unwary sucker. If you don't believe that, you have only to wait and watch it happen."

Val Gregory lashed out angrily. "That's a lot of hot air. I say give the drovers their way. They're about the only ones that come in my place, and goddamnit, I don't mean to bite the hand that feeds me. You think about it a minute and most of you'll see that you're rowin' the same boat."

Perry Tuttle, the dancehall impresario, readily agreed. But the others evidenced less certainty, mut-

tering and shaking their heads as they tried to unravel
what seemed a very tangled web. Seth Mabry, still
covered with grime from the smithy, pounded a meaty
fist into the palm of his hand.

"No, by God, I don't agree. It's like the judge says.
You give in to 'em, and make Bill Bailey marshal,
and we'll wind up presidin' over a wake."

"That's right," Sam Horner growled. "Inside of a
month they'd tear this town down around our ears."

Charlie Hoff and John Hamil, whose stores were
south of the tracks, both chimed in with quick support. That seemed to shift the scales off center, and
for a minute everybody just stood around and glared
at one another.

Harry Lovett, who operated the Gold Room, finally
sounded a note of moderation. "Seems to me we're
all after the same thing. It's just a matter of how we
get it. Hell, nobody wants to rankle the Texans. Most
of my business is with highrollers, but I still turn a
nice profit on the cowhands. The long and the tall of
it boils down to one thing. We can't operate in a town
where every store and saloon and dancehall has to be
its own law. That'd be like fightin' a fire with a wil-
low switch. There just wouldn't be no stoppin' it.
What we need is somebody the drovers respect. Just
between us, I don't think Bailey's the man."

The gambler had presented a convincing argument,
and before anyone could object, Bob Spivey came out
swinging. "Harry, you hit the nail right on the head.
Only I'd take it a step farther. What we need is not
so much a man they respect, but a man they're afraid
of. We've got the same problem Abilene had, and
everybody here knows how they solved it. Bear River

Tom Smith and Wild Bill Hickok. Texans are like any other jackass. You can't reason with 'em and being nice to 'em is a waste of time. You've got to teach 'em that every time they step out of line somebody's gonna get a busted skull. That's the only thing they understand."

The men stared back at him, somewhat dumbstruck by his heated tone. Spivey wasn't a violent man, and when he used words that strong it seemed prudent to weigh them carefully. None of them said anything simply because there was no way to refute his statement. It was all true.

After a while Val Gregory grunted and gave him a wry look. "I suppose you just happen to have a man in mind?"

Spivey walked to the door, yanked it open, and gestured to someone in the saloon. There was a brief wait and a slight stir of expectancy, but it came as no great surprise when McCluskie entered the office.

"Boys, I think you all know Mike McCluskie." Spivey slammed the door, and while everybody was still nodding, he gave them another broadside. "Mike, if we was to appoint you city marshal, how would you go about handlin' the Texans?"

McCluskie saw no reason to mince words. "Same as I would a mean dog. Educate 'em as to who's boss. That'd likely mean some skinned heads, and maybe even some shootin'. But it's the only thing that'd get the job done."

"What about the Santa Fe?" Perry Tuttle asked. "Wouldn't think they'd hold still for you gettin' mixed up in a thing like this."

"I cleared it with 'em this afternoon." The Irishman

nodded at Spivey. "Soon as Bob put it to me I got on the telegraph."

Sam Horner rubbed his jaw and looked thoughtful. "Where would you start? Educatin' the Texans, I mean."

McCluskie smiled. "Best way to kill a snake is to cut his head off."

The room went still and Spivey glanced around at the solemn faces. "Anybody opposed?"

When none of the men offered objection, he pulled out a badge and pinned it to McCluskie's shirt. Then he sighed wearily and a grave smile touched the corners of his mouth.

"Marshal, I guess you better get to killin' snakes."

TWELVE

McCluskie wasted little time. What he had in mind depended not so much on nerve or guts or even luck. It required mainly an element of surprise. The Texans had to be taken off guard, hit fast when they least expected it. But if it was to work he had to make his move before the board members scattered and spread the word. Otherwise the chances of taking Anderson and Bailey unawares would be pretty well eliminated.

While Spivey and the board were still hashing it around, he excused himself and made a hasty exit from the Lone Star. None of them expected anything rash on his part—they were the kind that believed in coppering their bets—and it would never occur to them that he might go the limit strictly on his own hook. That gave him an edge of perhaps a quarter hour, certainly no more. He meant to use it to best advantage.

His advantage.

Turning south, he crossed the tracks past the depot and began checking saloons along the street. His plan was already formulated, had been since that afternoon, yet he wasn't fooling himself about the risks. It boiled down to one of two things. Brace Anderson outright or make an object lesson out of Bailey. The latter alternative seemed the slicker move. Dusting Bailey off would serve as warning, and it might just avert a showdown with Anderson and his crew. That was something he wanted to avoid if at all possible, for Anderson had the men and the guns to turn Newton into a battleground. Still, the plan fairly bristled with danger. There were simply too many unknowns. If he had guessed wrong, and Anderson decided to deal himself a hand, the fat was in the fire.

But in the end that's what life was all about. Get a hunch, bet a bunch. Logic might make a man rich, but it was no substitute for raw instinct. Not when the other players carried guns.

A fellow either backed his hunches or he folded his cards and got out. Yet a man who cultivated the habit of running really wasn't worth his salt. To himself or anyone else.

Tony Hazeltine had proved that.

McCluskie found what he was looking for in front of Gregory's Saloon. The hitchrack was crowded with horses bearing the Flying A brand, and among them was Anderson's chestnut gelding. Odds were that Bill Bailey wouldn't be far from his Texan friends on this night.

The Irishman paused outside the batwing doors and surveyed the house. Anderson and Bailey were standing shoulder to shoulder at the bar, and the room was jammed with cowhands. There seemed to be a contest of sorts taking place. Whoever yelled the loudest got the floor and tried to top the others with some whopper about the afternoon's chief sporting event. Though they had been at it for some hours, the stories seemed to get better the longer they drank, and there was no dearth of laughter. Apparently Hazeltine's one-man race was the favorite topic, with the stampeded voters running a close second, and every time someone launched into a fresh version it was greeted by raucous shouts from the crowd.

McCluskie slapped the doors open and walked in as if he had just foreclosed on the mortgage. Hardly anyone noticed him at first, but as he crossed the room a ripple of silence sped along before him. When he came to a halt in front of Anderson and Bailey the saloon went still as a graveyard.

Anderson leaned back against the bar and gave Bailey a broad wink. "Well, looka who's here, Billy. The holy terror hisself." Suddenly he blinked drunkenly and peered a little closer. "Goddamn my soul. Billy, I think that's your badge he's wearin'."

"Let's get something straight," McCluskie warned him. "I didn't come here lookin' for trouble with you or your boys. My beef is with Bailey. You stay out of it and we'll just chalk this afternoon up to one for your side."

"Sort of a Mexican standoff."

"Something like that."

"Maybe it don't suit me to let it ride. You're a feller that needs his wick trimmed, 'specially after today."

"Then we can settle it later. Right now all I want is Bailey. Course, you can step in if you like. There's nothin' I can do to stop you. But it's gonna start folks to talkin'."

Bailey finally caught the drift and got his tongue untracked. "Hugh, he's bluffin' again. Can't you see that?"

Anderson's gaze never left the Irishman. "What kind o' talk?"

"Why, the sort of stuff they're already sayin'. That one Texan hasn't got the sand to go up against a lawman by himself."

The saloon went deathly still. Anderson's face turned red as ox blood and for a moment he almost lost his steely composure. Then a tiny bead kindled back deep in his eyes and a crafty smirk came over his mouth. Turning sideways, he leaned into the bar and gave Bailey a speculative look.

"What about it, Billy boy? Think you can haul his ashes?"

Bailey swallowed hard. Every man in the room was watching him and he knew it. They had heard his brag for the past week, and Anderson's question now made it a matter of fish or cut bait.

"Hell, yes, I can take him. Won't hardly be no contest at all."

McCluskie moved while he had the advantage. "Bailey, you've got your choice. Get out of town or go to the lockup."

"Lockup? You're talkin' through your hat. I ain't broke no law."

"You were deputized and you broke your oath. That's good for about six months accordin' to Judge Muse."

Bailey's lip curled back and he launched himself

off the bar. Whiskey had given him a measure of false courage but it hadn't clouded his judgment. Somewhere deep in his gut he knew that if he touched his gun the Irishman would kill him. But in a rough and tumble scrap it might just go the other way. He was bigger and stronger and he'd never yet lost a barroom brawl. Nor did he intend to lose this one. Hurtling forward, he let go a haymaker that would have demolished a stone church.

Except that it never landed. McCluskie slipped under the punch and buried his fist in the Texan's crotch. Back in Hell's Kitchen, one of New York's grimier slums, Irish youngsters were educated at an early age in the finer points of survival. What he didn't know about dirty fighting hadn't yet been written. Though he would have preferred to kill Bailey, he felt a certain grim satisfaction that it was to be settled with fists.

The Texan jackknifed at the middle, and as his head came down McCluskie's knee met it in a mushy crunch. Bailey reeled backward, his mouth and nose spurting blood, but he didn't go down. He was hurt bad, blinded by a chain of explosions that felt like a string of firecrackers inside his skull. Yet, in the way of a wounded beast, the pain only compounded his rage. Spitting teeth and bright wads of gore, he waded in again, flailing the air with a windmill of punches.

McCluskie gave ground, ducking some of the blows, warding off others. But he was hemmed in on all sides by shouting cowhands and there was no way of avoiding the burly Texan altogether. The air suddenly seemed filled with knuckles and for every punch he slipped past another sledgehammered off his head. With no room to maneuver, he had little choice but to absorb punishment and wait for an opening. His eyebrow split under the impact of a meaty fist and blood squirted down over his face. All at once it dawned on him that he was in grave danger. If he ever went down Bailey would stomp him to death, and the longer the fight lasted the more likely it was to happen. He had to end it fast or there was every chance he wouldn't end it at all. Operating now on sheer reflex, he stopped thinking and let his body simply react.

Shifting and dodging, he feinted with a left hook and suckered the Texan into a looping roundhouse right. The blow grazed past his ear and he slipped under Bailey's guard. Setting himself, he put his weight behind a whistling right that caught the other man squarely in the Adam's apple. Bailey's mouth flew open in a strangled gasp and his lungs started pumping for air. Both hands went to his throat and he doubled over, wretching in a hoarse, grating sound as he sucked for wind. McCluskie stepped back, planted himself, and kicked with every ounce of strength he possessed. The heel of his boot collided with Bailey's chin and the big man hurtled backward as if shot from a cannon. Cowhands scattered in every direction as the Texan went head over heels through the batwing doors and collapsed in a bloody mound on the boardwalk. Like a great whale snatched from the ocean's depths, he gave a blubbery sigh and lay still.

He was out cold.

McCluskie retrieved his hat, jammed it on his head, and somehow made it to the door without falling. He slammed one wing of the door open and leaned against it for support, inspecting the battered hulk with the cold, practiced eye of a mortician. Then he turned, glowering back at the crowd until his gaze came to rest on Anderson.

"When he comes to, give him the word. If he's not out of town in two hours he goes in the lockup."

The door swung shut behind him and he lurched off in the direction of the hotel. Except that he was walking, he would have sworn that somebody had just beaten the living bejesus out of him. Even his hair felt sore.

Kinch was stretched out on the bed with his hands locked behind his head. When McCluskie entered the room he gave him a sullen glance and looked away. Then it hit him, and he sat bolt upright, staring slack-jawed at the Irishman's eyebrow. The cut itself was crusted over with dried blood and didn't look so bad. But a knot the size of a hen egg had swollen his brow into an ugly, discolored lump.

McCluskie gave him a tight grin and headed for the washstand. "You're gonna catch lots of flies if you leave your mouth hangin' open."

The kid's clicked shut and he bounded out of bed. "Holy jumpin' catfish! What'd you do, butt heads with a steam engine?"

"Just about. Closest thing on two legs anyhow."

McCluskie sloshed water into a washbowl and then dampened one end of a towel. Inspecting himself in the mirror, he understood why the kid looked so startled. The lump over his left eye was the color of rotten squash and a jagged split laid bare the ridgebone along his brow. It was a souvenir he wouldn't soon forget. The same as his busted nose and scars from other fights. From the looks of this one, though, it would turn out to be a real humdinger.

After squeezing the towel out he began scrubbing caked blood off his face and mustache. The wound itself he left untouched. It had stopped bleeding and the flesh seemed pretty well stuck in place. Washing it now would only start the whole mess bubbling again. Ugly as it was, it would have to do for the moment.

Kinch came around and took a closer look at the cut. For a while he just stared, saying nothing, then he whistled softly under his breath. "Mike, that's clean down to the bone. Doc Boyd's the one that oughta be workin' on it, not you."

McCluskie grunted, swabbing dried blood out of his ear. "I'll let him patch me up later."

"Yah, but cripes, that thing needs stitchin'. You're hurt worse'n you think."

"Bud, I can't spare the time now. It'll have to wait."

The boy glanced at him in the mirror, struck by a sudden thought. "It was Bailey, wasn't it?"

"All five hundred pounds of him."

"What happened?"

"He beat the crap out of me, that's what happened. I finally got in a lucky punch and put him to sleep."

"C'mon, I'll bet there weren't no luck to it at all. You could take him with one hand strapped down."

The Irishman met his gaze in the mirror. "Much as I hate to admit it, that's one bet you'd lose."

Kinch blinked a couple of times, clearly amazed. "Tougher'n you thought he was?"

"Well, let's just say he wasn't exactly what you'd call a creampuff. Fact is, if I had it to do over, I'd sooner fight a real live gorilla. Probably stand a better chance all the way round."

"Quit funnin' me. You whipped him, didn't you?"

"Just barely, sport. Just barely."

McCluskie stripped off his shirt and tossed it in a corner. Crossing the room, he opened a dresser drawer and selected a fresh shirt. His arms and chest were covered with splotchy bruises from the pounding he'd taken, and every movement was a small agony in itself. Slipping into the shirt even made him wince, but as he turned back to the kid he forced himself to smile.

"Never seen it fail. Clean shirt and a little birdbath and it'll make a new man out of you every time."

"Malarkey!" Kinch obviously wasn't convinced. "The way that eye's puffed out, I'd say you need a sawbones more'n anything else."

"All in good time, bud. There's a few things that still need tendin' before I call it a night."

"You mean Bailey? I thought you said you whipped him."

"Some folks might give you an argument on that." McCluskie finished buttoning his shirt and began tucking it in his pants. "Thing is, I posted him out of town. Now I've got to make it stick."

The boy gave him a look of baffled aggrievement. "You knew it was gonna happen, didn't you? Even before you went down and talked with Spivey and his bunch, you knew you was gonna take that badge and go after Bailey and then start cleanin' house on the Texans. That's the way you had it figured all along, wasn't it?"

"Yeah, I guess it was. So what, though? You're talkin' like it was some skin off your nose."

"Damn right it is! You got me locked up in this room instead of lettin' me pitch in and help. That ain't my idea of what friends are for."

"Don't say ain't."

"Aw, horseapples. I'm serious and you're standin' there grinnin' like it was some kinda joke."

"Nope, it's a long ways from being a joke. Fact is, things are gettin' sorrier and sorrier. Regular as clockwork, too."

"You're gonna go lookin' for Bailey tonight, aren't you?"

McCluskie smiled and shook his head. "Most likely he's already left town. I'll just sashay around a while and see what's what."

"I'm goin' with you," Kinch announced.

"Some other time, bud. Tonight's liable to get a little dicey."

"Goddamnit, Mike, you got no call to treat me that way. I don't need nobody to wipe my nose. That's what you said, wasn't it? Out here a man's got to look after himself. Well I'm as fast as you are and I'm near about as good a shot, too."

"There's more to it than that. I've told you before, tin cans don't shoot back."

"Yeah? Well what if you go lookin' for Bailey and them drovers back his play? Where'll you be then?"

"That's the luck of the draw. A man has got to play whatever hand he's dealt. But that don't change nothin'. Like it or lump it, you're still not invited."

Kinch's eyes went watery all of a sudden, like a scolded child, and it was all McCluskie could do not to reach out and touch him. The kid was right. He didn't need anyone to wipe his nose. But for all the wrong reasons.

The last couple of days had been the hardest of the Irishman's life. After considerable self-examination he'd decided he didn't like what he saw in himself. Or what he'd done to the kid. Before he got to Newton, Kinch had been a decent, God-fearing youngster. Raised up proper, taught right from wrong. Innocent as a lamb if a man got down to brass tacks. Now he had himself a gun and somebody had showed him how to use it. Worse than that, though, he no longer had any qualms about using it. That *somebody* had drilled him so good he was all primed and ready to pop. Like a puppy that had been fed raw meat and gunpowder till he just couldn't wait to bust out and kill the first thing that moved.

Not that he wanted to kill anybody. Or even liked the idea. But just so he could prove to his teacher that he was everything a man ought to be. Cold and unfeeling and pitiless. The badge of manhood that had been drilled into him by someone who saw life at its very elemental worst.

The quick and the dead.

McCluskie wasn't proud of himself. Not any longer. He hadn't done the kid any favors, and that was an itch he'd have to learn to live with. But it was no longer just a matter of the kid killing someone. It had worked down to someone wanting to kill the kid. That was the one thing he wouldn't allow to happen.

However much he had to hurt the boy's feelings.

Watching him now, McCluskie made it even stronger. "Let's get it straight. You don't budge out of this room tonight. Got me?"

"Aw, c'mon, Mike." Kinch's look changed from one of hurt to disappointment. "I got a date with Sugar."

"What time?"

"Eight. I set it up with Belle yesterday."

The Irishman flipped out his pocket watch and gave it a quick check. "Okay. Just to Belle's and no-where else. I'll walk you down there, but I want you to leave that gun here."

"Cripes a'mighty, don't you never give up? How am I gonna look out for myself if you make me walk around naked?"

McCluskie was forced to agree. It was just possible that Bailey hadn't left town. That he might be laying for the kid somewhere, hopeful of settling at least one score before he made tracks. Even with a gun the kid would be in a bad fix. Without it he wouldn't have the chance of a snowball in hell.

"You got a deal. But remember, just Belle's. No-where else. Okay?"

Kinch grinned and gave him a shrug more elaborate than words.

After dropping the kid off at Belle's the Irishman headed for Hide Park. He hadn't spotted any of Anderson's horses along the street, which meant the Texan and his crew had probably adjourned to the sporting houses. Wherever they were that's where Bailey would be. If he was still in town. Oddly enough, he halfway wished Bailey had lit out for parts unknown. It would set his mind at rest about the kid.

But it wasn't a hope he meant to stake his life on. Wherever possible he stuck to the shadows, passing lighted windows quickly, without bothering to peek inside. Hitchracks were what interested him, and at the corner of Second and Main, he found what he was looking for. The same bunch of Flying A cow ponies, Anderson's chestnut included, standing hipshot in front of Tuttle's Dancehall.

Nearing the entrance, he slowed and moved up cautiously. If Bailey was inside he wanted to know precisely where, and more importantly, the best way to approach him. Otherwise, it was walk in blind and take a chance on getting his head shot off. Edging closer to the door, he stuck his head around the corner and slowly scanned the dancehall. Anderson's men were plainly visible, stomping and howling as they swung the dollar-a-dance girls around the floor. But Bailey himself was nowhere in sight.

Then, as his gaze swept the room once more, the door frame above his head splintered and an instant later he heard the snarl of a slug. Dropping and rolling, he came up on one knee as another shot chunked into the wall behind him. He saw Bailey across the street, scuttling along the boardwalk, firing as he ran. McCluskie drew a bead, waiting, enjoying it. The bastard had set him up like a duck in a shooting gallery. And it would have worked, slick as a whistle, except that the numbskull couldn't shoot worth a lick.

When Bailey silhouetted himself against the window of Krum's Dancehall, the Irishman opened fire. The first slug nailed him in his tracks, and the next two sent him crashing through the window in an explosion of sharded glass. When he collapsed on the floor inside only the soles of his boots were visible over the windowsill.

McCluskie uncoiled and came to his feet. There was considerable commotion inside Krum's and the thought of it made him chuckle. It wasn't every day that a dead man came sailing through the window. Not even in Hide Park. He was halfway across the street when the kid's voice rang out in a hard, businesslike growl.

"Hold it! First man that moves gets drilled."

The Irishman wheeled around, dropping low in a crouch as he brought the Colt to bear. Hugh Anderson and most of his crew were framed in the spill of light from the doorway of Tuttle's. Bunched together, they stood still as church mice, looking pretty sheepish in the bargain. Kinch had them covered from the side, over near the corner of the building.

McCluskie didn't know whether to laugh or curse. Somehow neither one seemed appropriate, so instead he just shook his head in mild wonderment. Plain to see, the kid had snuck out of Belle's and covered his back the whole time he was pussyfooting down the street. Like as not, the little wiseacre had it planned all along. But it proved one thing nobody was likely to question any more.

The kid had grit, clean through.

Chuckling to himself, McCluskie turned and started back across the street.

"Keep 'em covered, bud. I'll have a looksee and

make sure our friend is out of his misery."

Kinch just grinned and kept his pistol trained on the Texans. There wasn't any need to answer.

It had all been said.

THIRTEEN

McCluskie got the word over his second cup of coffee. Seated in the kitchen, watching Belle slap together some bacon and eggs, he was congratulating himself on last night's little fracas. It had been a nice piece of work. Bailey laid out on a slab and the Texans sent packing. That was one Anderson and his boys could paste in their hats and think about while they were out herding cows. Letting a slick-eared kid get the drop on them. They'd be a long time living that down.

Sweet Jesus! It was a sight to warm a man's heart. The way the kid had stood there, grinning, holding that Colt steady as a rock. Just like if someone had run up and primed his pump, he'd have hauled off and spouted a pail of ice water. Nervy didn't hardly describe it. The kid was ironclad and brass-bound. More guts than a bulldog with a new bone.

The thought brought his mind back to Belle. Last night had been something extraordinarily special. Maybe she was so glad he'd come out alive she just naturally put her heart into it. But whatever the reason, he felt like he'd been put through the wringer and hung out to dry. The lady knew what pleasured a man, and she flat turned into a wildcat once she came unwound.

Like this breakfast. Belle Siddons hadn't cooked a meal in all the time he'd known her. Hell, maybe never. But here she was, bustling around the kitchen, cursing every time the bacon grease spit the wrong way, determined to make this a very special day for him. All because he'd come through last night with his hide still intact.

He smiled and suddenly winced, reminded that his hide wasn't exactly intact after all. The swelling over his eye had gone down a bit, but he could scarcely stand to blow his nose. If he ever sneezed, he was a goner for sure.

That was more of Belle's doing. Pitching a fit till he'd agreed to let Doc Boyd stitch him back together. That old quack had the touch of a butcher, and with a needle he was nothing short of a menace. Still, the eyebrow was back in one piece, and seemed to be healing, so he had little room for complaint. Actually, he couldn't blame anybody but himself.

He should've learned to duck better.

Reflecting on that bit of wisdom, he had just started on a second cup of coffee when the kid burst through the door. He was breathing hard, as if he'd been running, and as he slammed to a halt before the table it suddenly caught up with him. He began to choke and a moment later his lungs gave way. McCluskie grabbed a bottle of whiskey and in between coughs forced a jigger down his throat. The liquor took hold slowly, trickling down through his system, and after a few more heaves and shudders, the spasm petered out. Gulping wind, blinking furiously to clear his eyes, the kid began sputtering in a hoarse, wheezing rattle.

"Slow down, goddamnit!" McCluskie barked. "The world's not comin' to an end. Just take your time, for chrissakes."

His gruff tone brought a withering look from Belle, but she didn't say anything. Bacon and eggs now forgotten, she moved around the table and eased Kinch into a chair. The boy nodded, still sucking air, and made a game attempt at smiling. Presently his color returned, and he seemed to have caught his breath, but his voice was still shaky.

"Mike, they're after you. It's all over town." He gasped and took another long draught of wind. "Soon as I walked into the cafe ever'body and his brother started givin' me the lowdown."

"Bud, you're not makin' sense. Who's after me?"

"The Texans. That's what I'm tryin' to tell you. They sent word in this mornin'."

"What d'ya mean, sent word? Who to?"

"I don't know. But it's all up and down the street. They aim to run you out of town or kill you. Cause of what you did to Bailey."

"Now is that a fact?" McCluskie tilted back in his chair and pulled out the makings. "Y'know, I always heard that pound for pound a Texan would assay out to about nine parts cowdung. Maybe we'll just find out before the day's over."

"You thickheaded Mick!" Belle squawled. "That's

just what you'd do, isn't it? Sit there and wait for them to come kill you."

"Cripes, Belle, what d'ya want him to do?"

Kinch gave her the look men reserve for hysterical women. "He can't back down or his name'd be mud."

"Sport, you hit it right on the head!" The Irishman slammed his fist on the table so hard his coffee mug bounced in the air. "Once a man runs he's got to keep on runnin'. You mark what I tell you. Them Texans are all hot air and taffy. Anybody that gets hisself in a swivel over that needs his head examined."

"Men!" Belle stamped her foot and glared down on them. "There's no end to it, is there? Just have to go on proving how tough you are."

McCluskie put a match to his cigarette and gave her a wry grin. "Belle, I don't like to bring it up, but you're burnin' my breakfast to a cinder."

Belle screeched and turned back to the stove. Kinch and the Irishman exchanged smiles as she commenced slinging smoking skillets in every direction. Just then the door banged open and Dora, the colored maid, came rushing in. The whites of her eyes were flared wide and she was waving a scrap of paper in her hand.

"Miz Belle! Miz Belle! Some man near broke the door in an' tol' me to give this to Mistah Mike. Said it was a mattah o' life and death."

Sugar raced into the kitchen before the others had time to collect their wits. "What's all the commotion about? Honest to Christ, Dora, you could wake the dead." All of a sudden she stopped and glanced around uneasily. "Well land o' Goshen, why is everybody staring at me like that?"

McCluskie took the piece of paper from Dora's hand and unfolded it. Inside was a scrawled message, and as he started reading the others scarcely dared to breathe. Finished, he flipped it on the table and let go with a sour grunt.

"Seems like Mr. Spivey has called a meetin' of the Town Board. Says for me to get up there pronto."

The room went still as a tomb and everyone just stared at him for a moment. Sugar gave a rabbity little sniff and wandered over behind Kinch. She leaned down and put her arms around his neck.

"Sweetie, what's going on? Everybody looks like they've just come from a wake."

Kinch took her hands and drew her down closer, but he kept his eyes on the Irishman. After a while McCluskie climbed to his feet and gave Sugar a grim smile. "Little lady, you're pretty close to right. Only thing is, the wake's just gettin' started."

"Sure'n begorra, the great Mick has spoken." Belle shot him a scathing look. "Now why don't you take a peek in your crystal ball and tell us who the corpse will be."

"Why Belle, that's simple," McCluskie grinned. "He'll be wearin' big jingly spurs and a ten-gallon hat, and after they kick all the dung out of him, they're gonna bury him in a matchbox."

"Very funny," Belle snapped. "I suppose you do song and dance, too."

"Just on request. Weddings and funerals and such. But in your case, I'll make an exception. Like tonight, maybe."

He chucked her under the chin, still smiling, and headed for the door. Then, struck by a sudden thought, he turned and looked back. "Say, you still keep a greener around the house?"

Belle stiffened and her eyes went wide with alarm. "What—what do you want with a shotgun?"

"Why, hell's bells, I didn't get no breakfast, that's what. Thought I might scare up a covey of birds on my way uptown."

"With buckshot?"

"There's all kinds of birds, honey. Some are just bigger'n others, that's all."

Belle moved past him without a word and stepped into the hall. She opened the door of a linen closet, reached inside, and pulled out a sawed-off shotgun. When she returned, McCluskie took it from her, broke it open, and checked the loads. Satisfied, he snapped it shut and thumbed the hammers back to half-cock. Looking up, he smiled, trying to lighten the moment.

"Jesus, I hope you never have to shoot this thing. With what you weigh a ten-gauge would knock you on your keester."

Her eyes went glassy with tears and she turned away. The others watched on in frozen silence, struck dumb by the Irishman's jovial manner. Sugar and Dora couldn't make heads or tails of the whole affair, but the look on Belle's face sent cold shivers racing through them. The girl clutched tighter at Kinch, as if some unseen specter might suddenly snatch him away.

The kid pushed her hands off and started to rise. Then he caught McCluskie's eye and slumped back in his chair. "I guess I don't have to ask. You want me to stay here and suck my thumb."

"Sport, you're gettin' to be a regular mind reader."

The Irishman smiled, but there was something hard about his eyes. "If that's not plain enough, lemme give it to you straight. You pull another stunt like last night and I'll swap ends on this scattergun and paddle your rump. Savvy?"

Without so much as a backward glance, he wheeled about and marched off down the hall. The sound of his footsteps slowly faded and moments later they heard the front door slam shut.

Kinch just sat there, grinding his teeth in quiet fury, while Sugar stroked his hair with the soft, fluttering touch of a small bird.

The shotgun didn't draw a crowd, but all along the street people rubbernecked and gawked as if the circus had come to town. McCluskie's appearance brought them out of stores and saloons like flies to honey, and as he strode past they gathered in buzzing knots to discuss this latest wrinkle. Word of the Texans' threat had spread through town only within the last hour, but already the gamblers were giving six-to-five that the Irishman wouldn't run. His tight-lipped scowl, and the double-barreled greener, seemed to reinforce those odds substantially.

Far from running, it appeared McCluskie had declared war.

The sensation created by his passage left the Irishman grimly amused. There was nothing quite like a killing, or better yet the chance of a massacre, to bring the fainthearts out of their holes. Not that they wanted to risk their own necks, or in any way get involved. They just wanted to watch. It spoke eloquently of man's grubby character.

But while he ignored the townspeople, Mc-

Cluskie's eyes were busy scanning the street. Oddly enough, the hitchracks stood empty and there wasn't a cowhand in sight. That in itself was a sign. More ominous, perhaps, than the warning delivered to Spivey.

Passing Hamil's Hardware, he noted that the doors were locked, and at the next corner Hoff's Grocery was also closed. Plain to see, the buzzards had come to roost at their favorite watering hole. Probably squawking and bickering among themselves while they waited for him to rout the bogeyman and lay all ghosts to rest.

Cursing fools and fainthearts alike, he crossed the tracks and headed for the Lone Star.

When he came through the door of Spivey's office the talk ground abruptly to a halt. The room was filled with smoke, and a sense of something queer, not as it should be, suddenly came over him. The men gathered there stared at him with eyes that were flat and guarded, and as his gaze touched their faces, he saw part of it. Apprehension and alarm and maybe even a little panic. Yet there was something more. Something he couldn't quite put his finger on. Mistrust, perhaps, or just a tinge of hatred. Whatever it was, it eluded him, and for the moment he set it aside. He shut the door but advanced no farther into the room. Someone coughed, and as if the spell had been broken, he nodded to Spivey, who was seated behind the desk.

"I got word you wanted to see me."

"Well, not just me, Mike." Spivey smiled and waved his hand at the others. "The boys here thought you ought to sit in on this. Sort of kick it around and see where we stand."

The rest of the men looked glum as undertakers, and Spivey's smile was far short of convincing. McCluskie felt the hair come up on the back of his neck. "Kick what around?"

"This goddamn mess you've got us in!" Perry Tuttle snarled. "What the hell'd you think we'd be meetin' for?"

The Irishman looked him over with a frosty scowl. "Mister, lemme give you some advice. Talk to me civil or don't talk to me at all. Otherwise you'll wind up with a sore head."

"Judas Priest, what'd I just get through tellin' you not ten minutes ago?" Val Gregory threw his cigar to the floor and glared around at the other men. "You can't say *boo* to him without gettin' your skull caved in. Or shot dead. Hell, it's no wonder the Texans are on the warpath."

"Gentlemen, please!" Judge Muse stepped to the center of the room, motioning for silence. "We have enough trouble on our hands without fighting among ourselves."

"You can say that again," Sam Horner muttered. "What beats me is why you go on jabbering about Texans. Newton's dead as a doornail anyway." His glance flicked around to the Irishman. "Case you haven't heard, we lost the referendum. Wichita will get its railroad."

Everyone fell silent, watching for his reaction. He let them stew for a minute, then pursed his lips. "Sorry to hear it."

"Yeah, sure," Perry Tuttle rasped, "we can see you're all broken up."

"Tuttle, I warned you once. Don't make me do it again."

"For Chrissakes, can't you fellas stick to one problem at a time?" Harry Lovett sounded as exasperated as he looked. "That railroad's a year down the line. Today's right now, and I'm a sonovabitch, it seems to me we ought to be thinkin' about the Texans."

"You're right, Harry. Dead right." Spivey looked over at the Irishman, but he was no longer smiling. "Mike, we got ourselves some powerful trouble this time. Anderson sent one of his boys in with a message. Short and sweet and to the point. Either you're on the noon train or they'll kill you and burn Newton down to the ground. I don't think they're foolin' either."

McCluskie shrugged, his expression wooden, almost detached. "Maybe. Leastways they might try. But they won't get very far."

"What makes you so sure?"

"This." McCluskie raised the shotgun, and in the closely packed room it was like looking down a cannon. "Double-ought at close range has a way of discouragin' a man."

"Who're you kiddin'?" Gregory inquired acidly. "Puttin' a couple of loads of buckshot into that crowd'd be like spittin' on a brush fire. Hell, there'll be a hundred of 'em. Maybe more."

"So you can hire yourself a new marshal. Thing is, they won't do nothin' to the town. That'd bring the army down on 'em, and not even Anderson's that dumb."

Judge Muse hawked and cleared his throat. "Mike, I'm afraid that's a risk some of these men feel they can't afford to take."

McCluskie sensed it again, the queer feeling that had come over him when he'd entered the room. "Care to make that a little plainer?"

"Yes, I suppose it's time. Understand, there is nothing personal in this. It's just that we have to consider what is best for the town."

Spivey broke in. "Mike, what he's tryin' to say is that we're between a rock and a hard place. If we keep you on, the Texans are gonna pull this town up by the roots."

McCluskie gave him a corrosive stare. "What you're sayin' is that I'm fired—"

"Now I didn't say that, Mike."

"—and if I don't hightail it you'll throw me to the wolves."

"Damnit, you're puttin' words in my mouth. Fact is, I don't know what we'd do without you. We're damned if we do and damned if we don't."

"If you wanted another Tonk Hazeltine that's what you should've hired." The Irishman tapped the badge on his shirt. "As long as I'm wearin' this it's up to me to pull the fat out of the fire. I'll handle Anderson and his bunch my own way. You boys just get yourselves a good seat and sit back and watch. It'll be worth the price of admission."

He turned to leave but the judge's voice brought him up short. "Mike, before you go, let me ask you one question. You have every right to get yourself killed. That's your privilege. But if you face that mob of Texans other people will get caught in the crossfire.

Now, do you really want the blood of innocent by-standers on your hands? Won't you agree that's rather a high price to pay for one man's pride?"

McCluskie just glared at him and after a moment the judge smiled. "I suspect you're too decent a man to take that chance. And it's not like you were running. I mean, after all, once things have calmed down there's nothing to stop you from coming back."

"Judge, that's the trouble with this world. There's too many runners and not enough stayers. Looks to me like it's time somebody drew the line."

The door opened and closed, and the men were left to ponder that cryptic observation. Nobody said anything, but as the silence deepened they found it difficult to look one another in the eye.

Belle gave a little start and jumped from her chair as he entered the parlor. Kinch and Sugartit also came to their feet, but none of them said a word. The dark rage covering his face was unlike anything they had ever seen, frightening in the way of a man touched by the sun. He stalked across the room and halted in front of Belle, thrusting the greener at her.

"Guess I won't be needing this after all."

"I don't understand." She took the shotgun, staring at him numbly. "What happened?"

"Spivey and the Judge just informed me that they don't want a war. Seems like Anderson sent word for me to be on the noon train and that bunch uptown don't know whether to blink or go blind."

Belle clapped her hands with delight. "Then you're leaving! You're really leaving."

"Hell, no, I'm not leavin'. Wild horses couldn't get

me out of here now. I'm just gonna give 'em a little war instead of a big one."

"Oh, God." She seemed to wilt and slumped back into her chair. "There's just no end to it. No end."

She let go of the shotgun and McCluskie grabbed it before it hit the floor. "That's where you're wrong. I mean to end it once and for all. Anderson's about to find out he treed the wrong town."

He hefted the greener, studying it a moment, then laid it across the table. "If I meet 'em without this, I've got an idea I can keep it between him and me. Thought it all out on the way back down here. That way Spivey and his bunch will just get that little war I was talkin' about."

"Mike McCluskie, you're a fool." Belle's lip trembled and she looked on the verge of tears. "Do you know that? A stubborn, thickheaded fool!"

Over her shoulder he saw the kid watching him intently and he smiled. "Well, it takes all kinds. Course, the nice part about being a fool—"

"—is that they walk in where angels fear to tread." Belle gave him a withering look. "Isn't that what you started to say?"

The kid blinked a couple of times, as if he couldn't believe what he was hearing. "Cripes a'mighty, he can't just take off like a scalded cat. Them Texans would be tellin' it all over that they scared him out of town. Then where'd he be?"

"Kinch Riley, you stop that!" Belle snapped. "He'd be alive, that's where he would be. If he doesn't get on that train they'll kill him. Is that what you want?"

"Stay out of it, Belle." McCluskie shot her a harsh look, then glanced back at the kid. "You're right, sport. Sometimes a fella does a thing just because it needs doing. That's what separates the men from the boys. Knowin' when to stop talkin' and get down to business. That's the kind of lingo Anderson will understand."

Belle uttered a small groan and sunk lower in her chair. "Talk never killed anybody. Or running either. If you weren't so pigheaded, you'd see that."

"Better a live coward"—McCluskie grinned—"isn't that how it goes?"

She turned away from him and began dabbing at her eyes with a handkerchief. Sugartit moved up behind the chair and laid a comforting hand on her shoulder. The Irishman stood there a moment, aware now that he'd gone too far with the jest. Then he glanced up and saw a look of fierce pride in the kid's eyes, and suddenly it was all right.

"Like I said, it's a thing that needs doing."

FOURTEEN

Newt Hansberry waited on the platform as the evening train rolled to a halt. This was the last train of the day, and the station master felt a weary sense of relief that it was only an hour late. All too often it was midnight or later before he closed the depot, and he was grateful for any small favors the Santa Fe passed along. Hansberry waved to the conductor as he stepped off the first passenger coach, then turned and headed toward the express car. Once he had the mailbag locked away he could call it a day and begin thinking about himself for a change. Heading the list was a good night's sleep, something that had been rare as hen's teeth since he took over in Newton.

Out of the corner of his eye Hansberry saw something that suddenly made him forget late trains and mailbags and even his weary bones. He wheeled around and peered intently toward the street. Just for a moment he thought his eyes were playing tricks on him. The flickering light from the station lamps was poor at best, and shadows often fooled a man into

seeing things that weren't there. Then he took a closer
look and grunted. What he saw wasn't imagination,
and it had nothing whatever to do with shadows. It
was the real article. A yard wide and big as life.

The station master couldn't seem to collect his
wits, and he just stood there as the Irishman crossed
the tracks and headed toward the southside. Before
he could call out it was too late. McCluskie melted
into the darkness at the end of the platform and vanished from sight. Hansberry blinked and rubbed his
eyes, looking again. There was something spooky
about it. Like waking from a dream bathed in sweat.
Yet there was nothing unreal about this, or the sudden
chill that swept along his backbone. It was just
damned hard to accept, and perhaps frightening in a
way he didn't wholly understand.

McCluskie got much the same reaction from people he passed on the street. Particularly the Texans.
They stopped, hardly able to credit their eyes, and
stared after him with a look of bemused disbelief.
That he hadn't quit and run, boarding the noon train,
they could accept. Some of them, the ones with
gumption, liked to believe they would have done like-
wise. But that he was out prowling the streets—fully
aware of what he faced—was beyond reason. The act
of a man who had crossed the line separating fool-
hardiness from common ordinary horse sense.

Angling across Main, McCluskie hesitated before
the hotel and then walked on. With everybody staring
at him like he was some kind of tent show freak, he
wasn't about to give them that satisfaction. They
could guess and be damned, but his reasons for staying were his own. He meant to keep it that way.

The baffled expression of everyone along the street gave him a moment of sardonic amusement. Before the night was out they would have talked themselves dry trying to put a label on it. But they wouldn't even come close, and in a grim sort of way, it made everything easier knowing he had them stumped. Most of them would chalk it up to lunacy or pride, and they weren't far wide of the mark. Perhaps, after all, it did take a certain brand of madness to stand and fight. To shoulder the burden of an entire town and accept the responsibility of the cheap piece of tin pinned on his shirt.

But there was a simpler truth, one not so readily apparent, and only after considerable thought had he seen it for what it was. *Each man in his own way feared certain things worse than he feared death itself.* The lucky ones were never forced to take that close a look at themselves, and what it was they feared most went to the grave with them. The vagaries of fate being what they were, McCluskie hadn't been that fortunate.

He had found his secret fear in the eyes of a kid.

That revelation had come hard, after searching his innermost self with a fine probe. Somehow it was all jumbled together. The town and the kid. Since the war he hadn't given a tinker's damn for anyone or any place. A nomad answerable to no one but himself, with no ties to bind him and no obligations he couldn't sever on the whim of the moment. Now, after grappling with it most of the day, he knew that it was only partly pride, and an even smaller sense of duty, which had prompted him to goad the Town Board. To back them into a corner and force them to let him stay and fight their fight. Underneath it all, perhaps overshadowing his own flinty pride, was the kid. That was the part which had come clear and crystal bright.

Quitters finished last.

Kinch had proved that in the siege with his own special devil. After all that had passed between them, McCluskie could do no less. The look he'd seen in the kid's eyes, exultant at his determination to stay and fight, had made it all worthwhile.

Whatever happened.

Along with a fitful day, holed up in Doc Boyd's office, this newly acquired awareness hadn't given him much rest. Which struck him as neither odd nor unreasonable. Somehow it seemed merely fitting. Luckily, he wasn't forced to dwell on it any longer.

Approaching Third, he saw the yellow parlor house and his thoughts turned to Belle Siddons. While he had curbed the impulse to stop at the hotel, there was no reason to avoid Belle. She was the closest thing he'd ever had to a sweet tooth, and tonight seemed a little late in the game to start resisting temptation.

When he entered the parlor, Belle uttered a small gasp and the color drained from her face. Several Texans were lolling about making smalltalk among themselves, and the conversation fell off sharply as he stepped through the doorway. Apparently they were passing time, waiting, for there wasn't a girl in sight. Somewhat taken aback, the cowhands stared at him as if he had dropped out of a tree. None of them said anything, but they suddenly got very careful with their hands. Galvanized at last, Belle came out of her chair as if touched by a hot poker.

She grabbed his arm, raking the Texans with a

fiery glance, and marched him through the door and down the hall to the kitchen. Only after she had drawn the shade on the back door did she turn on him. Somehow, though it came to him only at that moment, McCluskie had always liked her best when she was angry. She was plainly in one of her spitfire moods right now and the look on her face made him smile.

"Mike, for God's sake, stop grinning at me like a jackass. Don't you know what's happening?"

"Yes, ma'am." He doffed his hat and gave her a half bow. "You see I heard stories about this lady that snorts fire like a dragon, and I've come to pay my respects. Queer thing is, them stories weren't the least bit exaggerated."

"Stop it! Stop it!" A tear rolled down over her cheek and her bottom lip trembled. "They're going to kill you. Do you hear me, Mike? Anderson and his men are in town right now. This very minute. Don't you understand that?"

He crossed the kitchen and took her in his arms, sobered by what he had seen in her face. She met his embrace with a fierce hug and buried her head against his chest. After a moment he raised her chin and kissed her, slowly and with a gentleness he'd never shown before. When their lips parted, she gave a small sniffle and he smiled, wiping a tear off her cheek.

"There's lots of things I understand better than I did this morning."

Belle kissed his hand, then blinked as the words slowly took hold. "Why do you say that?"

"Well, I guess because I had plenty of time to do

some thinkin'. I've been holed up in Doc's office all day, waitin' for things to cool down before I braced Anderson. Just sat there starin' at the wall for the most part, figuring things out."

"What things?"

McCluskie let her go and drew back. He pulled out the makings, trickling tobacco onto paper, and started building a smoke. There was something deliberate and unhurried about his movements, as if he was stalling for time, keeping his hands occupied while he collected his thoughts. Belle waited him out, and at last, when he had the cigarette going, he met her gaze.

"I was thinkin' about the kid."

She gave him a quick intent look. "Kinch? Why, there isn't any reason to worry about him. He's just a boy. Texans aren't even low enough to take their spite out on a boy."

"That wasn't what I meant, just exactly." The Irishman took a deep drag and exhaled, studying the coal on the tip of his cigarette. "I was thinkin' about the way he looked at me this mornin' when he heard I hadn't quit."

"My god!" Belle paled and her eyes widened with comprehension. "You stayed so he would go on thinking you're some kind of holy terror."

"Something like that. I'd already made up my mind anyway, but it came to me sort of gradual that I stayed for the kid as much as for myself."

"And you're going to hunt Anderson down just to prove it?"

"That's about the gist of it, I guess." McCluskie flicked ashes toward the stove and smiled. "Seems odd, don't it? Can't say as I've quite gotten used to the idea myself."

"Not odd, Mike. Insane. Do you hear me? Crazy mad! You'll get yourself killed for nothing." She waited for an answer but he just stared at her. "He's dying, Mike. Don't you understand? In a few months he'll be dead and whatever you proved to him won't mean a thing."

"That's the point I've been tryin' to make. It'll mean a whole lot." His brow wrinkled and he took a swipe at his mustache. "Funny thing is, it's hard to explain, but when you get it boiled down, it's real simple. The kid don't have much besides me. When his string runs out I'd like to think nothin' between us had changed."

"You're just kidding yourself, don't you know that? He's in Sugar's room right now. Does that sound like someone who's all busted up because his idol might wind up dead?"

"Belle, you've been in the business long enough to know better'n that. Sugar's like a toy, just something to keep him from suckin' his thumb. Case you don't know it, he spent most of the day searchin' all over town for me. Doc told me so himself."

He took a final puff and ground out the cigarette in an ashtray. "You say he's in her room now?"

"Yes, has been for the last hour. Why?"

"Nothin'. Just hadn't planned on seein' him, that's all."

"Well that takes the cake! I'll swear to God, it does."

"What's the matter?"

"Matter? Oh, nothing at all. Just that you're willing

to get yourself killed, but you can't face Kinch and tell him why. Doesn't that strike you as a little strange?"

"Depends on how you look at it. First off, it's not all because of him. Never was. And there's no sense makin' it out to be something it's not. Next thing is, I don't plan on gettin' killed. Likely there's some that could punch my ticket, but Anderson's not one of 'em."

He paused and gave her a tight grin. "Tell you the truth, there's an even better reason. Hell, you know how the kid is. If I told him what's up, he'd raise a fuss to go along. I want him kept out of it."

"You're crazy, Mike McCluskie, do you know that?" Belle stomped off a couple of paces and turned, glaring at him. "Just once in your life couldn't you stop being so bullheaded? Anderson isn't about to stick to some silly set of rules. He wants you dead, and he'll use every dirty trick in the book to make sure it comes out that way."

The Irishman shrugged and grinned. "I'm not much for playin' by the rules myself. Like the fella said, there's more'n one way to skin a cat."

"Whose cat you gonna skin?"

Startled, they looked around and saw Kinch standing in the hallway door. There was no way of knowing how much he had overheard, yet it was apparently enough. His eyes were fastened on McCluskie, and as he stepped into the kitchen, a wide grin spread over his face.

"You've been sorta scarce today. Everybody said you was hidin' out, but I told 'em they was full of beans. I knew you'd show up."

"Well you had me shaded there, bud. I wasn't real sure myself till the sun went down."

"Yeah, but I knew. I got to thinkin' about it after you left this mornin', and I told myself there wasn't nothin' on earth that'd stop you. I was right, too."

"Guess you were, at that." McCluskie smiled and punched him on the shoulder.

Kinch paused and eyed him steadily for a moment. "You're gonna go lookin' for Anderson, aren't you?"

The Irishman cocked one eyebrow and nodded. "Guess it's time somebody called his hand. Seein' as I'm still wearin' the badge, it might as well be me."

"You'll need some help. Like that night with Bailey, remember? Wouldn't hurt none a'tall for me to back your play."

"Not this time, bud. It's personal. Something Anderson and me have got to settle ourselves."

McCluskie expected the kid to sull up and start pouting. Oddly enough, it fell the other way. Kinch nodded, as if he understood perfectly, and for once showed no inclination to argue the matter. They stared at one another a while and the Irishman finally chuckled.

"Tell you what. You wait here for me and after I'm finished we'll go up and check the yards together. Fair enough?"

"Whatever you say," the boy agreed. "Don't make it too long though. I'd like to get back to Sugar sometime tonight."

McCluskie laughed and turned back to Belle. She was fighting hard, determined not to cry, and from somewhere, she dredged up a tiny smile.

"Take care, Irish."

He grinned and gave her a playful swat on the rump. "Keep the lamp lit. I'll be home early."

"I'll be waiting."

Her words had a hollow ring, and as he entered the hallway she couldn't hold back any longer. Tears sluiced down over her cheeks, and when the front door slammed her heart seemed to stop altogether. Behind her another door closed softly, eased shut with only a slight click of the latch. Somehow she knew even before she looked, and a spark of hope fanned bright as she spun around.

Kinch was gone.

McCluskie had thought it all out at Doc Boyd's while he waited for it to grow dark. The choice was between Gregory's Saloon and Perry Tuttle's Dancehall. Those were Anderson's favorite hangouts, and sooner or later he was bound to show. Tuttle's somehow seemed the more appropriate of the two dives. That was where he had killed Bailey, and it was only fitting that the big dog himself be accorded the same honor.

Striding along toward Hide Park, the Irishman amused himself with a wry thought. Chances were it wouldn't be so much a matter of him finding Anderson as it would of Anderson finding him. While he had been on the street less than an hour, it stood to reason that word had already spread through town. The Texan likely knew every move he was making, and by now any chance of surprise would have worn off. The fact that he chose to flaunt his decision by invading Tuttle's made it a challenge Anderson could hardly overlook. That was something he counted on heavily. Bait of sorts.

Only in this case it was a tossup. He hadn't quite decided whether he was the hunter or the hunted. Not that he would have too long a wait to find out. The question would be resolved soon enough.

Tuttle's was packed to the rafters and going full blast when he came through the doors. He swept the room with a slow look, assuring himself that Anderson wasn't present, but even that seemed more out of habit than any sense of caution. Tonight he didn't feel wary. Quite the opposite, he felt reckless and anxious to have it done with. He had come here to kill a man, and the sooner it could be arranged the better. Perhaps he wouldn't walk away himself, but that had ceased to trouble him. For an assortment of reasons, none of which he had bothered to explore, he was riding a crest of fatalism. It was a thing that needed doing and he had tapped himself for the job. That was explanation enough.

Spotting an empty table against the far wall, he began threading his way through the crowd. That was an edge of sorts—having his back against a wall—and it might just make the difference. At least they couldn't get him from behind. Approaching the table, he noted that the one next to it was occupied by two Santa Fe men. An engineer, Pat Lee, and his fireman, Jim Hickey. When they glanced up, he shook his head, warning them off, and slipped into a chair on the far side of the table.

He ordered a bottle and when it came, poured himself a single shot. Leaning back in his chair, he sipped at the whiskey and kept one eye on the door while he watched the mad whirl on the dancefloor. The trailhands turned the whole affair into one big struggle, pushing and shoving and shouting, like a gang of wrestlers who just happened to wear spurs and six-guns. Their antics alone were worth the price of admission, and in passing, it occurred to him that dancehall girls earned every nickel of their money. After a night on the floor with the Texans, most of them were probably nothing short of a walking bruise.

McCluskie was still nursing the same drink when the doors flew open and Hugh Anderson strode into the room. Behind him were five hard-looking cowhands, and they all came together in a little knot, quickly scanning the crowd. One of the hands spotted him sitting alone at the table and nudged Anderson. The Texan's gaze jerked around, settling on him at last, and an instant later the men separated. Anderson came straight toward him, but the others fanned out and moved across the floor from different directions. The Irishman grunted to himself, smiling slightly, and climbed to his feet.

Now he had his answer. It was the hunters who had come for him. Which was just as well. He'd never been one to bet short odds, anyway.

Anderson stopped before the table, his lip curled back in a gloating smirk. "Mister, you got enough brass for a whole herd of monkeys."

"Want to borrow some?"

"Come again?"

"Why, it's pretty simple, Anderson." The Irishman jerked his chin at the five hands. They were now spread out in a rough crescent that had him caught in a crossfire from all sides. "If you had the starch to fight your own fights you wouldn't need so much help."

"You stupid sonovabitch. This ain't no church social. That plain enough, or you want me to draw you a picture?"

McCluskie started to answer but movement off to the left caught his eye. The moment his gaze flicked in that direction he knew he'd been suckered. The cowhand farthest down the line had shifted positions, distracting him for a crucial instant, and it had worked perfectly. Even as his eyes swung back he sensed it was too late.

The gun in Anderson's hand was out and cocked, pointed straight at him. It was as if time and motion had been arrested. He saw the hammer fall, glimpsed the first sparks of the muzzle flash, and then went stone blind as the pistol exploded in his face. The slug mushroomed through his throat, slamming him back against the wall, and he felt something warm and sticky splash down over his shirt. Then his knees buckled and he was suddenly gripped with the urgency of killing Anderson.

The trainmen seated at the next table leaped to their feet just as the other Texans opened fire. The shots were meant for the Irishman, but they were hurried and wide of the mark. Lee collapsed, drilled through the bowels, and Hickey screamed as a slug shattered the thigh bone in his right leg. McCluskie heard the gunfire and the terrified shrieks of dancehall girls, sensed the crowd scattering. But it was all somehow distant, even a little unreal. Blinded, falling swiftly into darkness, he willed his hand to move. To finish what he had come here to do.

Another bullet smacked him in the ribs, but like a dead snake, operating on nerves alone, his hand reacted and came up with the Colt. That he couldn't see Anderson bothered him not at all. In his mind's eye he remembered exactly where the Texan was standing, and even as he pressed the trigger, he knew the shot had struck home.

Anderson staggered backward, jolted by a fiery blow in the chest. His legs gave way and he started falling, but with some last reserve of strength he raised his pistol. The floor and his rump collided with a jarring crash, and in a final moment of consciousness, he shot the Irishman in the back.

McCluskie grunted with the impact of the slug and pitched headlong between the tables. His leg twitched and his hand slowly opened, releasing its grip on the Colt. Then his eyes rolled back, the sockets empty and sightless, and he lay still. A wispy tendril of smoke curled out of the gun barrel and disappeared. Afterward there was nothing.

Hurriedly, the five cowhands moved forward and gathered around their boss. The instant they came together the sharp crack of a pistol racketed across the dancehall. One of them clutched at his stomach and slumped forward, and the crowd again dove for cover. But the Texans seemed frozen in their tracks, unable to move, staring at the fallen man in a numbed stupor.

Standing just inside the doorway, Kinch thumbed the hammer back and fired again. There was nothing rushed in either his manner or in his soft feathering of the trigger, yet the shots thundered across the room in a staccato roar. Coolly, just as the Irishman had taught him, he spaced the shots evenly and drilled each one precisely where he meant it to go. Every time the worn Navy bucked, another Texan went down, and within a half-dozen heartbeats it was over. When the gun clicked at last on an empty chamber not a single cowhand was left standing.

The kid slowly lowered his arm and stood there a moment, looking at the tangled jumble of bodies. Something inside tugged at him, demanding that he cross the room and make sure. But he shook it off, touched by the grim certainty that there was no need. He had seen McCluskie go down, felt that last slug as if it had been pumped into his own back. Whatever the Irishman had been in life, he was just a dead man now. Nothing more. That wasn't the way Kinch wanted to remember him.

Backing away, he holstered the Colt and brushed through the doors. There was a sudden chill in the air and he shivered. Then he knew it for what it was and hurried on into the night.

FIFTEEN

The kitchen was still as a crypt. Kinch sat slumped in a chair, elbows on his knees, staring at nothing. He hadn't moved in the last hour, as if he had retreated within himself, locked in some private hell all his own.

Seated nearby, Sugartit looked on helplessly. She wanted to touch him, take his hand, comfort him in some way. But she knew there was nothing she could say or do that would ease his grief. Years ago she had lost her own family, and she remembered all too well the cold, deadened sensation that clutched at a person's heart. Remorse came quickly, but it released its hold with infinite slowness. Only time would heal the feeling of rage and loss that gripped him now, and difficult as it was to remain quiet, the girl merely watched and waited. When he was ready, in his own fashion, Kinch would find some way to talk about it. However long it took, Sugar meant to be there when he needed her.

The only sound in the room was the soft shuffling

of Belle's footsteps. She circled the kitchen like some
distracted ghost, wan and ashen-faced. She had long
since cried herself out, and now she felt drained of
all emotion and feeling. Her hands were icy cold,
though the room was sticky with summer warmth,
and she kept her arms wrapped around her waist.
Somehow she couldn't bring herself to take a seat at
the table. She felt some restless compulsion to keep
moving, almost as if in her mindless pacing she could
outdistance the dreaded truth.

That he was gone, lying dead at that very moment,
she still couldn't accept. He had always been so
charged with life, full of strength and wit and energy,
and it just wasn't possible. Someone with his lust and
vitality simply couldn't be extinguished that easily.
Like snuffing out a candle. Whatever God watched
over Irishmen wasn't that capricious or impersonal.
To cut a man down in his prime, kill him needlessly
and without purpose, was a waste she couldn't comprehend. A truth so appalling her mind simply
wouldn't accept it as fact.

Yet she had known it the minute Kinch walked
through the door. The sickly pallor covering his face,
and the shock etched deep in his eyes, bespoke the
horror of what she had feared most. Stunned, unwill-
ing to believe, she had stared at him a long time, until
finally he lowered his head. His words still rang in
her ears.

"They got him."

That was all he said. Having spoken those simple
words, a death knell sounded in a quavering voice, he
slumped into a chair and hadn't moved since. A rush
of tears stung her eyes, and something vile and thick

clogged her throat. She hadn't questioned him then, and later, after she stopped crying, it didn't seem to matter. Whatever had happened, she chose not to hear it. Somehow, in a way she hadn't yet reconciled, if she didn't hear it then it couldn't be true. But even as she witlessly paced the floor, frantically seeking to elude the truth, she knew deep down that she was only fooling herself.

Mike McCluskie was dead, and all the King's horses and all the King's men couldn't bring him back again.

The nursery rhyme jarred her to a halt.

Humpty Dumpty sat on a wall. Humpty Dumpty had a great fall. *God, she must be going mad*. Reaching back into her childhood, dredging up some silly nonsense to cushion a blow she hadn't yet been able to accept. That's what it was. Some form of lunacy. Letting her mind play tricks on her. Turning a tall, sandy-haired hellraiser into a dumpy little innocent. Watching him tumble from the wall and shatter to pieces. It was a device. A childish game. Something conjured up from God knew where to convince herself that he really couldn't be scraped up and glued back together again.

Life didn't work that way. Only in fairy tales did the good guys win. Out in the harsh reality of the world it was the bastards who walked away with the marbles. They never died. Or perhaps, because there were so many of them, it merely seemed that their numbers never dwindled.

She turned and was amazed to see Sugartit sitting beside the boy. Though her mind seemed lucid and clear, she couldn't recall the girl entering the kitchen.

But obviously she had, and plain to see, she was wholly absorbed in the boy's sorrow. Then, in a moment of self-loathing, Belle realized that for the past hour she had dwelt on nothing but her own grief. She had given no thought whatever to Kinch. Wasted and sickly, dying by inches as some ravenous thing consumed his lungs, he sat there stricken with remorse. Not for himself, but instead for what he had lost. The one man who had befriended him, given him a reason to live, made him forget for a small moment in time that he was marked for an early grave.

All at once she felt an outpouring of pity that completely overshadowed her own misery.

She crossed the room and gently laid her hand on the kid's head. "Mike wouldn't like this. Do you know that? If he walked through the door and caught us moping around this way, he'd just raise holy hell."

Kinch kept his eyes fastened on the floor. "He ain't comin' through that door no more."

"No, I suppose not." Belle's stomach churned, queasy and fluttering, as if she had swallowed a jar of butterflies. She took a deep breath to steady herself. "But that's no reason for us to crawl off and call it quits. Mike lived more in thirty years than most men would in a couple of lifetimes. And he enjoyed every minute of it, too. Do you know what he would say if he was here right now? He'd laugh and then he'd say, 'Bud, it's nothin' but the luck of the draw. You pays your money and you takes your chances.' "

Sugartit placed her hand on the boy's arm. "Belle's right, honey. You mustn't blame yourself. These things just happen."

Kinch slammed out of the chair, jerking away from

them. "What d'you know about it? You weren't there."

The girl winced as if she had been slapped in the face and stared after him in bewilderment. He stalked across the room and stopped beside the stove, refusing to look at them. The heat of his words left them startled, and for a while no one said anything. Sugartit had plainly hit a nerve, and the boy's wretched look disturbed them in a way they couldn't quite fathom.

Presently Belle got a grip on herself and decided to have another try. Whatever was bothering him had to be brought out into the open. Left to fester and feed upon itself, it would only get worse.

"Are you blaming yourself, Kinch? Is that why you can't look at us?"

He still wouldn't turn around. "I waited too long. I should've gone in there with him. If there'd been two of us they would've backed down."

"Don't you think Mike thought of that?"

"I dunno."

"Yes you do. You know it very well. He told you to stay here because he didn't want you mixed up in his business."

"Yeah, but he was always sayin' that. I shouldn't have listened."

"That's just the point. You didn't listen. You followed him anyway. Nobody could have asked any more of you than that. Why should you expect more of yourself?"

"She's right," Sugartit blurted. "You did what you could, and that's the most anybody can do."

"Cripes, you two don't understand nothin', d'you?

I should've talked him into lettin' me back his play. He'd have let me if I just spoke up."

"You're wrong, Kinch." Belle's tone had the hard ring of certainty. "He would have tied you hand and foot before he let that happen."

"Don't be too sure. He knew how good I was with a gun."

"Yes, but there's something you don't understand. He thought the sun rose and set in your hat. Why else do you think he stayed here? You just think about it a minute and you'll see he would never have let you go along."

Belle realized her mistake only after the words were out. She damned herself for speaking out of turn, but by then it was too late. Kinch whirled around, his eyes distended and flecked through with doubt.

"What're you talkin' about? It was his job. He stayed here to get Anderson, didn't he?"

"Of course he did. I just meant he thought too much of you to risk getting you in a jam with the Texans."

"That's not what you meant. You're lyin' to me, Belle." The kid scrunched his eyes up in a tight scowl. "I got a right to know, and you got no right to hold back on me."

She just stared at him a moment, feeling helplessly trapped. "Maybe you're right. I suppose when a man does something like that it shouldn't be kept a secret." She faltered, trying to break it gently, but found herself at a loss for words. "I don't know how else to say it except straight out. Mike never ran from anything in his life and he probably wouldn't have this time either. But there was more to it. The reason he stayed, I mean. He was willing to take on Anderson and that bunch so you wouldn't think bad of him. I tried to talk him out of it, but he had his mind set."

"Oh, Jesus." Kinch seemed to stagger and his face went ashen. "He didn't have to get himself killed to prove nothin'. I would've understood."

"Mike thought it was important enough that he wasn't willing to take a chance. He did it the only way he knew how." The boy was badly shaken, worse than Belle had expected, and she tried to soften the blow. "Maybe it's not much consolation, but Mike was sure he could trick Anderson into making it a fair fight. I think he really believed he could pull it off and walk away without a scratch."

"Yeah, it was fair awright." The muscle at the back of his jawbone twitched in a hard knot. "Six to one. With him backed up against a wall."

There was a sharp rap at the back door and the room went deathly still. Kinch's arm moved and the Colt appeared in his hand. Stepping back beside the stove, he drew a bead on the window shade, then nodded for Belle to open the door. She threw the bolt and jerked the door open, moving quickly out of the line of fire. Dr. Gass Boyd stepped through the entrance and stopped, looking first at the two women and finally at the gun barrel centered on his chest.

"Youngster, it would be a serious error in judgment for you to shoot me. I'm about the last friend you have left in this town."

Belle slammed the door and bolted it. Something in Boyd's voice alarmed her, more the tone than the words themselves. But as she turned to question him,

Kinch holstered his pistol and stepped away from the stove.

"Sorry I threw down on you, Doc. Guess I'm a little jumpy tonight."

"Save your apologies, son." Boyd set his bag on the table and smiled. "After what you did tonight you have every right to a case of nerves."

"I don't understand." Belle shot him a puzzled frown. "What's Kinch done?"

The doctor looked from her to the boy and one eyebrow arched quizzically. "You mean to say you haven't told them?"

"Just about Mike." Kinch ducked his head. "Didn't see that it'd do any good to tell 'em about the rest."

"What do you mean, the rest?" Belle moved around the table and faced Boyd squarely. "Doc, will you please explain what's going on here?"

"Perhaps you ladies had better sit down. Our young friend seems to have omitted a few rather salient details."

Sugar obediently took a chair but Belle remained standing. "Quit hedging, Doc. Let's have it."

"Very well. I have just come from the hardware store, which is temporarily serving as a funeral parlor. As of this moment there are five dead and four wounded. In my opinion one of the wounded will die before morning. The others have a fair chance of pulling through."

"You're still beating around the bush. What does that have to do with Kinch?"

Boyd glanced over at the kid and his sober expression deepened. "Belle, it seems you are harboring a paragon of modesty as well as a fugitive. According to a hundred or so eyewitnesses, Kinch personally accounted for four of the dead and two wounded. One of whom is as good as dead right now."

"Oh, my God." Belle sank into a chair.

Sugartit stared unblinkingly at the boy, her eyes glazed over with shock. Belle was aghast, unable to get her breath for a moment, and finally she looked up at the little physician in complete bafflement.

"He didn't say a word."

"Precisely." Boyd treated the kid to a benevolent smile. "Along with unerring aim, he has the virtue of modesty."

"Five men." Sugartit's statement came in a dazed whisper.

"And a sixth wounded," Boyd noted in a clinical undertone.

Belle shook her head in numbed disbelief, and at last her gaze settled on the boy. "Why didn't you tell us?"

Kinch gave her a hangdog look and shrugged. "I figured you had enough on your mind. Hearin' about Mike, I mean."

"But how in God's name did you do it?"

"I dunno. It all happened so fast I ain't real sure." The kid mulled it over a little, trying to sort it out in his mind. "Mike and Anderson went down just as I come through the door. Then the rest of them Texans ganged around for a looksee and I started shootin'. Funny thing is, they just stood there. Didn't try to run or duck or nothin'. It was sorta like knockin' over tin cans, the way Mike showed me when we used to practice."

Silence descended on the kitchen, and for a moment everybody stared at him in dumbstruck wonder. Presently the doctor cleared his throat and tugged reflectively at his ear. "I'm not much of a shot myself, but offhand, I'd say you had a damned good teacher."

"Best there ever was," Kinch agreed. They exchanged glances and the boy frowned. "Something you said bothers me, though, Doc. I ain't no slouch with a pistol, but Mike never taught me how to get six men with five shots. Y'see, he believed in carryin' the hammer on an empty chamber, and I only had five loads. That's what throws me. There was only five of them Texans and I drilled ever' one of 'em dead center."

Boyd eyed him speculatively. "What about the trainmen?"

"What trainmen?"

"There were two Santa Fe men seated at the table next to Mike's."

"I don't know what you're talkin' about, Doc. All I saw was that bunch of Texans standin' over Mike and Anderson."

Belle gave the physician a keen sidewise scrutiny. "Doc you're hinting at something. That's why you snuck in the back door, isn't it? You didn't want anybody to see you coming here."

"I'm afraid so," Boyd admitted. "One of those killed was Pat Lee, a Santa Fe engineer." He paused and looked at the boy. "Anderson swears it was your shot that killed him."

"Anderson?" Kinch spit the word out, glaring thunderstruck at the doctor.

"Why, yes. Perhaps I forgot to mention it, but Anderson is going to live. Despite a very serious chest wound he'll make it with any luck—"

Kinch kicked a chair out of his way and headed for the door. Boyd surprised even himself by darting across the room and blocking the boy's path.

"Now wait a minute, son. Don't go running off in circles like a bee had stung you."

"Get out of my road, Doc."

"You're going after Anderson, is that it?"

"Damn right! He killed Mike, didn't he?"

"And I suppose Mike taught you how to walk in and shoot a wounded man while he's laid up in bed. Was that one of the lessons?"

The kid just stood there a moment, half mad with rage, then he wheeled around and started pacing the kitchen. Belle and Sugar looked at one another, unnerved and not a little frightened by what they had seen in his face. After a moment Boyd regained his composure and came back to the table.

"Kinch, the night Mike McCluskie carried you to his hotel room I promised him I would look after your health. In a way, that's what I'm still doing. Now suppose we all remain calm and I'll explain what brought me down here."

When no one objected, he went on. "There are a number of things happening in Newton at this very moment. First off, Bob Spivey has telegraphed to Topeka for a U.S. marshal. He means to put the fear of God into this town, and there is already talk that a swift hanging would be just the thing to turn the trick. Secondly, Anderson's statement against Kinch is backed up by one of his cowhands. The one who's going to live. Son, from where I sit, that makes you the prime candidate for a necktie party."

Kinch stopped pacing and glowered back at him. "I didn't kill no Santa Fe men. All I shot was Texans."

"I don't doubt that for an instant. But it's your word against theirs. Now, you're in no danger from the Texans. From what I heard at the dancehall they don't think much of the way Anderson and his crew ganged up on Mike. Unfortunately, the same can't be said for the townspeople. Or the U.S. marshal, for that matter."

"What about Anderson?" the kid demanded. "Hadn't somebody better charge him with murder for what he did to Mike?"

"Probably they will. But from the little I've overheard, I suspect his men intend to sneak him out of town before morning. That won't change a thing, though. Anderson's statement will still hold, and when the U.S. marshal arrives, he'll come looking for you. Whether or not you actually killed the engineer would be a moot question at that point. The townspeople are in an ugly mood. They want to make an example out of somebody, and I'm afraid you're it."

The logic of Boyd's argument was hard to dispute. Everybody looked back and forth at one another for a while and there was silent agreement that the boy had worked himself into a bad spot.

At last Belle turned to face the doctor. "What you're saying is that we have to get Kinch out of town before some drunk gets busy and organizes a lynching bee."

"That's correct," Boyd nodded. "The sooner, the better. Oddly enough, there happens to be a horse out back right now. With a bill of sale in the saddlebags."

Belle turned her attention to the kid. "Kinch, I'll try to tell you what Mike would say if he was sitting here instead of me. He was a gambling man, but he always knew when to fold a losing hand. That's what you're holding right now. It's time to call it quits and find yourself a new game. Otherwise Sugar's liable to be burying her man the same as I'll have to bury mine."

That struck home and the boy swallowed hard. "Maybe so, but I'd feel like I'm runnin' out on Mike. I sorta had it in mind to finish what he'd started with them Texans."

"You're not running! Get that out of your head. If you had it to do over, you'd have told Mike to leave. Wouldn't you? Well this is the same thing. Sugartit and me, we're asking you to go for our sake."

Sugartit flew out of her chair and rushed into the kid's arms. "Please, honey, do it for me. Just this once. Wherever you go, you let me know and I'll be there with bells on. I promise."

Boyd cleared his throat and looked away. "Son, I suspect there's little time to waste. You had best be off while you have the chance."

"Yeah, sorta looks that way, don't it?"

Kinch pulled Belle into a tight hug and afterward shook the doctor's hand. Then Sugartit threw herself in his arms again and gave him a kiss that was meant to last. Finally she let go and he headed for the door. But halfway out he turned and looked back.

"You want to hear something funny? I ain't never been on a horse in my life. This oughta be a real circus."

The door closed and they just stood there staring at it. Somehow the whole thing seemed a bad dream of sorts. A nightmare that would pass with the darkness and leave their lives untouched. But moments later the spell was broken and reality came back to stay.

Hoofbeats sounded outside and slowly faded into the night. Like a drummer boy tapping the final march, they heard a faint tattoo in the soft brown earth.

Kinch Riley would return no more.

SIXTEEN

The kid often came to a grove of cottonwoods along the riverbank. There was something peaceful about the shade of the tall trees and the sluggish waters gliding past in a silty murmur. Yet it was only within the past week that the Red had settled down and started to behave itself. Spring rains had been heavy, and the snaky, meandering stream had crested in a raging torrent for better than a fortnight. A mile wide in some places, roiling and frothing in its turbulent rush southward, it had been a watery graveyard of uprooted trees, wild things dead and bloated, and a flotsam of debris collected in its wandering rampage.

Kinch hadn't cared much for the river in flood. It reminded him somehow of an angry beast, hungry and drooling, devouring everything in its path. Watching it had disturbed him, almost as if the river and the thing gnawing on his lungs were of a breed. Kindred in the way of things carnivorous and lurking and ever ready to fatten themselves on the flesh of the living. That the thought was far-fetched—a figment of the nagging fear which shadowed his thoughts these days—made little difference. It was no less real, and in some dark corner of his mind he was obsessed with but one thing.

He must not die. Not yet.

But as the flood waters receded, and the warmth of spring came again to the land, he found a measure of hope. The prairie turned green as an emerald sea, and overnight bright clusters of wild flowers seemed to burst from the earth. New life, borne in on soft southerly breezes, was everywhere he looked. He drew strength from its freshness and vitality, and with it, the belief that he might, after all, hold on till his work was completed.

While his thoughts still turned inward, he dwelled not so much on himself these days as on the happier times of a summer past. That brief moment when he'd had it all. The excitement and laughs, friendship and love. When the Irishman and Belle and Sugartit had given him something that neither time nor space could erase.

Seated beneath the leafy cottonwoods, soaking up the warming rays of a plains sun, his mind often wandered back. There, in a bright little cranny far off in his head, McCluskie still lived. Tall and square-jawed, alert and tough and faintly amused. Busted nose and all. Kinch could summon forth at will the tiniest detail. How the Irishman walked and talked and knocked back a jigger of whiskey. The hard-as-nails smile and the quick grin and that soft grunt of disgust. The deliberate way he had of rolling a smoke and flicking a match to life with his thumbnail. Every mannerism and quirk acquired on the long hard trail from Hell's Kitchen to the dusty plains of Kansas. It was all there, shiny bright and clear as polished glass, tucked neatly away in the back of his mind. Etched boldly and without flaw, indelible as a tattoo.

Still, the kid wasn't fooling himself. The image existed only in his mind's eye. Along with it persisted the certain knowledge that the man he summoned back so easily was dead and long buried. Mike McCluskie, that part of him which was flesh and bone, had been under ground some nine months now. The other part, what the preachers always made such a fuss over, was somewhere else. Though just exactly where, nobody had ever nailed down for sure.

Kinch had given that considerable thought. Particularly at night, when he came to sit beneath the trees and listen to the river. Head canted back, searching the starry skies, he wondered if there was a heaven. Or a hell. And if so, the further imponderable. Which place would the spirit of Mike McCluskie most likely be found? Somehow he had a feeling that the Irishman had made it to the Pearly Gates. Probably fighting every step of the way, too. Heels dug in and squawling like a sore-tailed bear.

The kind of people McCluskie had enjoyed most in life were the rascals and the highrollers. Being separated from them in the hereafter was something he wouldn't have counted on. If he had gone up instead of down, it had doubtless taken some mighty hard shoving on somebody's part.

Which way he had gone didn't mean a hill of·beans, though. Not to the kid, anyhow. He himself wasn't all that hooked on religion, and so far as he could see, one way looked about as good as another.

Just so he could tag along with the Irishman when his time came, he didn't give a tinker's damn whether it was heaven or hell or somewhere in between. When he checked out for good, finally gave up the ghost, he meant to make himself heard on that score. Anybody that tried to punch his ticket a different direction than McCluskie was going to have a stiff scrap on his hands.

Kinch chuckled to himself and slowly climbed to his feet. For someone living on borrowed time, he sure had some powerful notions about the hereafter. Like as not, when a fellow passed on, they just gave him his choice, and there wasn't any big rhubarb about it one way or another.

Squinting at the sun, he made it a couple of hours before noon. Time he got off his duff and swamped out the saloon. Quitting the cottonwoods, he headed up the bluff toward the station.

The town wasn't much. Aside from the saloon, there was a ramshackle hotel, two general stores, and perhaps a dozen houses scattered about the surrounding prairie. While the township had been officially designated Salt Creek, honoring a nearby tributary which flowed into the larger stream, it was known simply and universally as Red River Station. Situated on a high limestone bluff overlooking the river, it was as far as a man could go and still say he was in Texas. Once across the Red, he entered Indian Territory.

The reason for the station's existence lay just west of town. There, a wide natural chute, boxed in by limestone walls, sloped down to the water's edge. Starting in late spring and continuing into early fall, herds of longhorns were driven down the chute and pushed across the river. A sandbar ran out from the northern back, and when the cattle reached it, they had begun the long haul up the Chisholm Trail. Some two hundred fifty miles farther north, after passing through Indian Territory, the trail ended at the Kansas railheads. Abilene, Newton, and the reigning cowtown this particular spring, Wichita.

Small as it was, it seemed likely that Red River Station would thrive and prosper forever. Though the cowtowns faded into obscurity as quickly as rails were laid south and west, the station depended on nothing but itself. It was the gateway to the Chisholm Trail, the only known route through the red man's domain, and this strategic location guaranteed its prosperity.

The trail herds passing the station had been sparse thus far this spring. Cattlemen were reluctant to ford the Red, and the latticework of rivers crisscrossing Indian Territory, until the flood waters had receded. But the billowing plume of dust on the southern horizon steadily grew larger, and over the past week, better than three herds a day had made the crossing. Soon, as many as ten herds a day, numbering upward of twenty thousand longhorns, would be stacked up waiting their turn. Red River Station made not a nickel's profit off the cattle themselves, but its little business community grew fat and sleek off the cowhands. After fording the river, the Texans wouldn't again see civilization for close to a month. The station was their last chance, and in the way of thirsty men doing dirty work, they made the most of it.

Kinch came through the back door of the Alamo Saloon and started collecting his gear. Broom and featherduster, mop and pail. Tools of the trade for a swamper. He didn't care much for the job, emptying spittoons and swabbing drunken puke off the floor, but beggars couldn't be choosers. The way he looked at it, Roy Oliphant had been damned white to take him on, and he felt lucky to have a bunk in the back room, three squares, and a little pocket change. More importantly, it allowed him to straddle the jaws of the Chisholm Trail while he watched and planned and waited.

Hugh Anderson would pass this way, as did all Texas cattlemen, sooner or later. When he finally showed, the kid had a little surprise in store. An early Christmas present, of sorts.

After sweeping the floor, he started mopping the place with a practiced, unhurried stroke. Nine months on the end of a mop had taught him that there was no fast way. Slow and sure, that was the ticket. It left the floor clean and his lungs only slightly bent out of shape. He was nearing the rear of the saloon when Roy Oliphant came down from his room upstairs.

The boy paused, breathing hard, and leaned on his mop. "Mornin', Mr. Oliphant. All set for another day?"

Oliphant stopped at the bottom of the stairwell and gave him a dour look. The saloonkeeper was a gruff bear of a man, widowed and without children, and early morning generally found him foul-tempered and vinegary. But in his own way, rough and at times blistering, he had a soft spot for strays. The ones life had shortchanged and left discarded along the wayside. There were occasions when he reminded the kid just the least little bit of McCluskie.

"Bub, ever' now and then I get the notion you haven't got a lick of sense. Look at the way you're huffin' and puffin'. Goddamnit, how many times I got to tell you? Slow down. Take it easy. The world ain't gonna swell up and bust if you don't burn the end off that mop."

Kinch grinned and took another swipe at the floor. "Aw, cripes, Mr. Oliphant. Workin' up a sweat is good for me. Gets all the kinks ironed out."

"Why sure it does," Oliphant observed tartly. "That's why you're wheezin' like a windbroke horse, ain't it?"

"Well, I always say if a job's worth doing it's worth doing right. Besides, you got the cleanest saloon in town, so what're you always hollerin' about?"

Oliphant grunted, holding back on a smile. "Don't give me none of your sass. This here's the only saloon in town and you damn well know it."

"Yeah, but it's still the cleanest."

"Real funny, 'cept I ain't laughin'. You're not foolin' anybody, y'know?"

"What d'you mean?"

"C'mon, don't play dumb." Oliphant headed toward the bar, talking over his shoulder. "You buzzsaw that mop around so you can get back down to the bluffs and start bangin' away at tin cans."

The kid blinked a couple of times, but he didn't say anything.

Oliphant drew himself a warm beer and downed half the mug in a thirsty gulp. He wasn't a man who liked riddles, and the boy had been a puzzle of sorts from the day he walked through the door. Looking back, he often wondered why he'd taken the kid on in the first place. He knew galloping consumption when he saw it, and a smoky saloon didn't exactly qualify as a sanatorium. Which was what the youngster needed. When he rode into town, he'd been nothing but skin and bones, pale and sickly and wracked with fits of coughing. The saloonkeeper would have laid odds that he'd never make it through the winter. But the kid had hung on somehow, and never once had he shirked the job.

Still, after all these months, Oliphant had to admit to himself that he really didn't know the kid. Like this deal with the tin cans. He had sneaked down and watched the boy practice a few times. What he saw left him flabbergasted. Kinch made greased lightning look like molasses at forty below. Moreover, he rarely ever missed, and he went through the daily drills as if his life depended on every shot. The saloonkeeper was baffled by the whole thing, plagued by questions that seemingly defied any reasonable answer.

Where had he learned to handle a gun that slick? Who taught him? And most confusing of all, why in the name of Christ did he practice so religiously, day in and day out?

But Roy Oliphant wasn't the kind to stick his nose in other people's business. He ruminated on it a lot, watching silently as the kid spent every spare nickel on powder and lead, yet he had never once allowed his curiosity to get the better of him. Not until today.

Kinch was still staring at him as he drained the mug and set it on the bar. "That's what I like about you, bub. You're closemouthed as a bear trap."

"You mean the gun?"

"Hell, yes. What did you think I was talkin' about?

You work at it like your tail was on fire, but I never once seen you wear the damn thing. Sorta gets a fellow to wonderin' after a while."

"Aw, it's just a game somebody taught me. Y'know, something to help pass the time."

Oliphant gave him a skeptical look, but decided to let it drop. He hadn't meant to bring it up in the first place, and why he'd picked this morning to get nosy puzzled him all the more. Live and let live was his motto, and he'd never lost any skin minding his own business. If the kid had some deep dark secret, that was his privilege. Most times, what a man didn't know couldn't hurt him, and it was best left that way.

"Well, I guess you'd better finish up and get on back to your game. Only do me a favor, will you? Don't wear out my mops so fast. Them goddamn things cost money."

Kinch grinned and went back to swabbing the floor. Presently he disappeared into the storeroom and after a while the rusty hinges on the alley door groaned. Oliphant listened, waiting for it to close, then smiled and drew himself another beer.

Some more tin cans were about to bite the dust.

The kid's routine varied little from day to day. Swamp out the saloon, put in an hour or so working with the Colt, then return to his room and clean and reload the pistol. Afterward, he would stroll around town, always keeping his eye peeled for horses with a certain brand, and generally end up back at the saloon not long after noontime. There, he took up a position at the back of the room, supposedly on hand in case Oliphant needed any help. But his purpose in being there had nothing to do with the job. Whenever a fresh batch of Texans rode into town they made straight for the Alamo, and he carefully scrutinized each face that came through the door. While the long hours sapped his strength, and breathing the smoke-filled air steadily worsened his cough, he seldom budged from his post till closing time. Sooner or later the face he sought would come through the door, and he wasn't about to muff the only chance he might get.

Time was running out too fast for that.

Hardly anyone paid him any mind. He was just a skinny kid with a hacking cough who cleaned up their messes. That was the way Kinch wanted it. He kept himself in the background, and since coming to town, he had made it a habit to never wear a gun. With the Colt on his hip, there was the ever present likelihood he might become involved in an argument and wind up getting himself killed. That was one chance he wasn't willing to risk. Not until he'd performed a little chore of his own.

Yet there were times when he despaired of ever pulling it off, and this was one of those days. His cough was progressively growing worse, and the only thing that kept it under control was the bottle he had stashed in the storeroom. It was something to ponder. Nine months he had waited, and unless something happened damned quick, he'd cough once too often and that would be the end of it. Which wasn't what he'd planned at all, and personal feelings aside, it seemed unfair as hell to boot. Justice deserved a better shake than that. But then, as the Irishman had once observed, life was like a big bird. It had a way of dumping a load on a man's head just when he needed it least.

This was a thought much on his mind as he returned from the storeroom. He had developed quite a tolerance for whiskey the past few months, and the fiery trickle seeping down through his innards right now felt very pleasant. With any luck at all it would hold his cough at bay for a good hour. Not that an hour was what he needed, though. The way things were shaping up he had to figure out a cure that would hold him for a month, or more. Maybe the whole damn summer. Then he chuckled grimly to himself, amused by the absurdity of it.

There wasn't any cure, and if that big bird didn't dump all over him, he might just luck out with a couple of more weeks. But as he came through the door the laugh died, and his throat went dry as a bone.

Hugh Anderson and his crew were bellied up to the bar.

Kinch couldn't quite believe it for a minute. After all this time they had finally showed. He stood there, watching Oliphant serve them, and it slowly became real. The waiting had ended, at last, and for the first time in longer than he could remember, he felt calm and rested and cold as a chunk of ice. Stepping back, just the way he'd planned it, he simply vanished in the doorway and headed for his room.

Moments later, he reappeared and the Colt was cinched high on his hip. Walking forward, he stopped at the end of the bar, standing loose and easy, just the way the Irishman had taught him.

"Anderson."

The word ripped across the saloon and everyone

turned in his direction. Somebody snickered, but most of the crowd just gawked. The hard edge to his voice had fooled them, and they weren't quite sure it was this raggedy kid who had spoken. Then they saw the gun, and the look in his eye, and the place went still as a church. Kid or not, he had dealt himself a man's hand.

Anderson took a step away from the bar and gave him a quizzical frown. The Texan had slimmed down some from last summer, but other than that, he looked mean as ever.

"You want somethin', button?"

"Yeah. I want you."

"That a fact?" Anderson eyed him a little closer. "I don't place you just exactly. We met somewheres?"

"It'll come back to you. Tuttle's Dancehall in Newton. The night you murdered Mike McCluskie."

"Sonovabitch!" Anderson stiffened and a dark scowl came over his face. "You're the one that shot up my crew."

Kinch nodded, smiling. "Now it's your turn."

"Sonny, you done bought yourself a fistful of daisies."

"You gonna fight, yellowbelly, or just talk me to death?"

The Texan grabbed for his gun and got it halfway out of the holster. Kinch's arm hardly seemed to move, but the battered old Navy suddenly appeared in his hand. Anderson froze and they stared at one another for an instant, then the kid smiled and pulled the trigger. A bright red dot blossomed on the Texan's shirt front, just below the brisket, and he slammed sideways into the bar. Kinch gun-shot him as he hung there, and when he slumped forward, placed still a third slug squarely in his chest. Anderson hit the floor like a felled ox, stone cold and stiffening fast.

There was a moment of stunned silence.

Before anybody could move, Roy Oliphant hauled out a sawed-off shotgun from beneath the bar. The hammers were earred back and he waved it in the general direction of Anderson's crew. "Boys, the way I call it, that was a fair fight. Everybody satisfied, or you want to argue about it?"

One of the cowhands snorted, flicking a glance down at the body. "Mister, there ain't no argument to it. The kid gave him his chance. More'n he deserved, I reckon. Leastways some folks'd say so."

Kinch turned, holstering the Colt, and walked back toward the storeroom. His eyes were bright and alive, and oddly enough, his lungs had never pumped better. He felt like a man who had just settled a long-standing debt.

What the Irish would have called a family debt.

Late that afternoon Kinch stepped aboard his horse and leaned down to shake hands with the saloon-keeper. "I'm obliged for everything, Mr. Oliphant."

"Hell, you earned your keep. Just wish you'd have give me the lowdown sooner, that's all. Not that you needed any help. But it don't never hurt to have somebody backin' your play."

"Yeah, that's the same thing I used to tell a friend of mine." The kid sobered a minute, then he grunted and gave off a little chuckle. "He was sort of bull-headed, too."

"You're talkin' about that McCluskie fellow."

"Irish, his friends called him. You should've known him, Mr. Oliphant. He was one of a kind. Won't never be another one like him."

"Well, it's finished now. You ever get back this way, you look me up, bub. I can always use a good man." They both knew it wasn't likely, but it sounded good. Oliphant suddenly threw back his head and glared up at the boy. "Say, goddamn! I ain't ever thought to ask. Which way you headed?"

"Wichita. Just as fast as this nag'll carry me."

"That's a pretty fair ride. Sure you're in any kind o' shape to make it?"

"I'll make it." The kid went warm all over, and in a sudden flash, Sugartit's kewpie-doll face passed through his mind. "Got somebody waitin' on me."

Oliphant leered back at him and grinned. "Yah, what's her name?"

"Mr. Oliphant, you wouldn't believe me if I told you."

Kinch laughed and kicked his horse into a scrambling lope. Just as he hit the grade down to the river, he turned back and waved. Then he was gone.

One last time, he was off to see the elephant.